She needed desperately to feel alive...

That much Garrett knew when, on a sob, she ran into his arms.

"Kirsten..." He wanted to tell her it'd be over soon, but she knew better. Her body became curiously still against his, and he didn't know whether she'd given up or was trying to absorb his strength. The hours of having gone without talking to her son had worn too thin.

She finally pulled back to look into his eyes, but her focus went to his mouth and she brought her lips to his.

Garrett thought of nothing but answering her in kind. The sound she made blistered his soul. He opened his mouth and covered hers, drawing her into a kiss so deep, so replete with meaning, he could no longer discern a separation of their souls.

Kirsten was all he knew, all he'd ever wanted, more woman than he'd ever had or known. Still her own woman, still Christo's mother. And he was in love with her.

But could he keep her alive?

ABOUT THE AUTHOR

Carly Bishop's novels are praised for their "sensuality, riveting emotional appeal and first-class suspense" as one reviewer put it. She was a RITA finalist in 1996 for her Harlequin Intrigue novel *Reckless Lover,* and she's won numerous awards and critical acclaim throughout her ten-year writing career. Carly lives in Colorado and regularly uses the great Rocky Mountains as the backdrop in her stories.

Books by Carly Bishop

HARLEQUIN INTRIGUE

Don't miss any of our special offers. Write to us at the following address for information on our newest releases.

Harlequin Reader Service
U.S.: 3010 Walden Ave., P.O. Box 1325, Buffalo, NY 14269
Canadian: P.O. Box 609, Fort Erie, Ont. L2A 5X3

No Baby But Mine
Carly Bishop

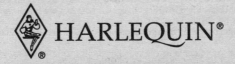

HARLEQUIN®

TORONTO • NEW YORK • LONDON
AMSTERDAM • PARIS • SYDNEY • HAMBURG
STOCKHOLM • ATHENS • TOKYO • MILAN • MADRID
PRAGUE • WARSAW • BUDAPEST • AUCKLAND

ISBN 0-373-22538-5

NO BABY BUT MINE

Copyright © 1999 by Cheryl McGonigle

This edition published by arrangement with Harlequin Books S.A.

® and TM are trademarks of the publisher. Trademarks indicated with ® are registered in the United States Patent and Trademark Office, the Canadian Trade Marks Office and in other countries.

Visit us at www.romance.net

Printed in U.S.A.

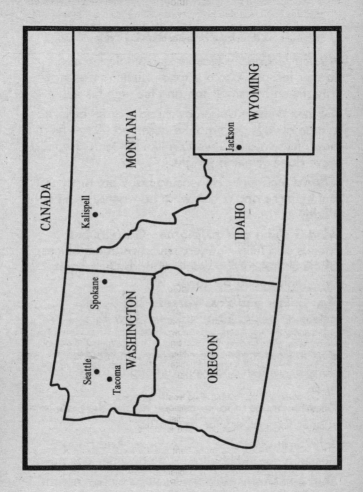

CAST OF CHARACTERS

Kirsten McCourt—Teacher and single mom, a former forensic photographer, Kirsten's past now threatened her small son and life with his father.

Garrett Weisz—Undercover cop Garrett believed a man always got what he deserved. A son he'd never known and a woman like Kirsten... He must have done something right.

Christo McCourt—He was no baby but Kirsten's, but by three and a half what he wanted was his daddy.

Matt Guiliani and JD Thorne—Garrett's best friends and fellow undercover cops in the offices of the U.S. Attorney would stand by him against any peril, bound by honor.

Ann Calder and Ross Vorees—The Seattle detectives had a lot at stake in Garrett's undercover operation.

Burton Rawlings—The attorney ran afoul of dangerous men and went running to Kirsten for help.

Chet Loehman—Some people had to die—some sooner than others for real justice.

John Grenallo—The U.S. Attorney had refused Kirsten a second chance. Why give her one now?

Sam and Ginny Wilder—Kirsten's closest friends gave Christo an unsafe haven.

Prologue

The stonecutters were behind in their labors.

It would be at least six weeks before Lane Montgomery's name and the dates circumscribing his life—his birth and death—would be carved in stone. The soothing voice commending her murdered husband to eternity droned on. But as Kirsten McCourt stood through the graveside service in the freezing rain, focused on the blank face of the granite marker, it was her own epitaph she imagined.

Should have known better…

Lane Montgomery had betrayed her, and it had cost her everything she held dear. Everything. Right up to the moment. She would have chosen to leave his burial to the state—whoever took care of burying the bodies of criminals and miscreants. But she hadn't been given the choice. The mourners were outnumbered by the undercover cops who had forced this graveside charade on the off chance that one of Chet Loehman's TruthSayers' vigilante bullyboys would attend. If nothing else, it was believed, but to thumb a nose at them all.

Deputy Assistant U.S. Attorney John Grenallo,

short, balding, holding a hat in his hands, stood across the casket from Kirsten. He knew her argument backward and forward, inside and out. She had a professional responsibility, an ethical obligation, and now a personal stake in battling back. She couldn't let Lane's betrayal go unanswered. She'd begged Grenallo for the chance to help rebuild the case against Loehman.

Grenallo had refused. He knew her desperate mood, knew what it would mean to her to be given the chance to earn back the trust and respect of her peers. But he couldn't do it. His office had been severely compromised; his own leadership in question, but this debacle all finally funneled down to her judgment, or lack of it, first personal, and then professional.

She was, more or less, the singular cause of the collapse of their undercover operation. If she hadn't fallen for Lane, hadn't believed his buttery-smooth lies, hadn't trusted faulty instincts, hadn't allowed him where he should never have been, the case against Loehman and the operation he ran would be in the bag now.

Reason told her Lane would have found another way if not through her. Logic even Grenallo espoused conceded the possibility. Lane Montgomery had been charged with document security throughout the Federal Building, and that included the photo files Kirsten had built up, the digital computer backups and the portfolios she'd prepared for trial.

But it was on her watch, in her wake, that the destruction had occurred.

Yea, though I walk through the Valley of the Shadow of Death...

For as long as Kirsten could remember, images captured on film had been her passion. Moments seized and held forever. But early on, the disparity she sometimes saw between the captive image and the truth laid bare the lie, so it wasn't to commercial photography that she'd turned, but to forensics.

She had a gift, a talent, a rare ability, no matter whether for photography or videography, for seeing in an image what was true and what was not. What accurately reflected the subject and what had been tampered with. And beneath her talent lay an even deeper, more abiding commitment to ferret out the lies and produce in her images evidence of the truth.

Kirsten McCourt was perfectly suited to her place in the judicial scheme of things. But since she should have known better, should have ferreted out the deceptions delivered with stunning accuracy and Lane's perfect pitch—to make her believe she was loved beyond measure—she was also perfectly positioned to facilitate her own downfall.

Still, she was not down for the count.

She was the daughter of a Boston cop who, after walking a beat for twenty years, had finally been promoted to detective—only to lose his wife in a gun battle in their own home. The death of Kirsten's mother hadn't stopped Fitz McCourt.

No way.

I will fear no evil...

Nothing would have stopped Kirsten, either. Not even this crushing loss of confidence. There were scapegoats, and then there were scapegoats, and she was one. But Grenallo's doubts not only dictated the end of her career, they echoed the judgment of her own heart. Should have known better.

The drizzle turned to pelting sleet and in the course of the brief ceremony, the somber gray Seattle skies blackened.

Surely goodness and mercy will follow me all the days of my life...

Or not.

THE MERCURY WAS a Seattle hot spot, a dance club built into the Marquis, a five-star hotel bordering the posh Seattle suburbs. Her room—for she would never return to the houseboat she had shared with Lane—was at the far end of the seventh story. But on the first floor, the deejays rocked all night long with seventies music, and on the second, the eighties.

She chose the first floor for the sheer distance in time from this dreadful night, and worked her way to a corner booth meant for two. Still dressed in her simple black sheath, she draped her coat over the back and sat sipping wine, trying to lose herself in the music until she was fairly certain she'd had one too many goblets of the warm, fragrant, sensual Bordeaux.

One too many wasn't enough yet, to compensate the losses.

She knew perfectly well that even if she managed to pass out cold, she would not reach that point.

She knew on a rational level that this was the epitome of bad decision making and poor judgment. Why not just buy a bottle and take it to her room?

She'd been hassled a couple of times by would-be Lotharios. She was getting hassled again, this time to dance. But anything, even this, was better than facing the awesome, impersonal silence of the hotel room she'd rented, where she could only think, *Should have known better.*

"C'mon, babe. Don't be a drag. Dance with me. Whatever's wrong, I'll make it right." The guy was big and drunk, his complexion florid, a beefy fist already reaching for her when he was interrupted by a tap on the shoulder from behind.

"Exactly what part of 'no' is a mystery to you, friend?"

Kirsten stared, wide-eyed, dumbstruck by all the wine, more by the hard-edged, impossible dark good looks and don't-screw-with-me tone of the man behind the man hassling her.

"Oh, Lordy-loo," the drunk snarled. "Look what we've got here. A han'some dude. A *friend.* A real hero."

"Hey! You kidding me?" Shouting over the music now, making light, in an instant the hero had gone from threatening to jovial. "You really don't remember?" The hero offered his hand to shake as if the two really were old buddies and the dull-witted drunk, confused now, reflexively stuck out his own oversize mitt to shake.

Kirsten really didn't get what happened in that handshake, but the big dumb drunk broke out in a cold sweat inside of a few seconds, and in a few seconds more, bowed out, mumbling apologies—or obscenities. Didn't matter. He was gone.

The hero was left standing alone over her small

table. She swallowed, shivered hard, and swallowed again to keep from asking him from her tipsy unguarded state if he knew what an utterly compelling nose he had. What an implacable jaw, intriguing cheekbones. What deep blue eyes, commanding forehead. She noticed those things, noticed the details and the bigger picture, what didn't fit, what suited so exquisitely.

He wore a suit that matched her sheath in degrees of mourning black, but his near-black burgundy tie hung slack, his cuffs undone, his stiff white collar unbuttoned. Dark hair, sparkling in the strobes, curled at the parted placket at his throat.

"I...um—" Her fingers fluttered to her own throat, to her hair. She tucked a strand behind her ear. The strobes flashed, neon streamed, the music rained down hard, the candle on the table flickered softly, but beyond this man, suddenly nothing else seemed real. "Thank you."

"You're welcome."

"Did you hurt him?"

His eyes never left her. She had no idea what color they might be. "His ego hurts more than his hand."

"Was that necessary?"

He blinked. "You tell me."

Her chin went up. "I could have handled it."

"That isn't exactly the point." Her wits felt so dulled she couldn't tell if he believed her or not. "Mind if I sit?"

"No." She did mind. She wanted to be left alone, but an objection wasn't what came out. He put down his drink, something dark and amber and undiluted, and sank loose-limbed into the booth. She had to move her knees to avoid the heat of his. "So, what is the point?"

"*I'm* offended when a woman has to deal with that kind of behavior."

"Oh, then you *are* a hero," she blurted, overcompensating because her foolish heart was going pit-a-pat. So smooth, so genteel-slash-rugged-slash-manly. So evolved. He was either a real hero or a more dangerous man to her by far than the drunk. With her history, she should know better. "That was really *very* good."

"Yeah, that's me." His smoky, dark voice painted images of broken glass. "Really very good."

"Whose hero are you usually?"

His amazing jaw cocked sideways. She blinked. Swallowed. Her head dipped low as she tried awfully hard to convince herself that it was wine impacting her impression that it was raw pain she saw in the sudden asymmetry, grief in the quirky angle. Her question had somehow come at him with the unwitting precision of a surgeon's scalpel. Was it the strobe revealing tears in his eyes, or only her imagination?

"I'm sorry. I didn't mean—"

"Sure you did." He swallowed in one long gulp the remains of the liquor.

"No, really. I'm an idiot for saying that. I just came from burying—"

"It's just that I buried my wife today."

"—my husband." Had she said that already, said

she'd buried Lane? "I've had too much too drink and— What did you say?"

"I said…" His jaw tightened again. The tears glittering in his eyes were no artifact of the light. "I said I buried my wife today."

"Oh my God, no—"

He shrugged. "Apropos of whose hero I thought I was." But his voice broke over the sarcasm like sea foam over the jagged reach of driftwood buried beneath the sand.

"I'm so sorry…"

He swore softly. His jaw locked. A tear spilled. His hands formed fists till his knuckles shone white.

She couldn't bear to watch him, couldn't take her eyes off him. She knew he hadn't heard her. It was on the tip of her tongue to repeat that she had buried her husband as well, to offer that sliver of comfort, of empathy. *I know what you're going through. I'm there. I'm going through it, too.*

But she wasn't. Her emotions were of another ilk.

She knew by the unguarded flicker of pain over his features that his grief had only to do with an unendurable loss very unlike hers, owing nothing to shame or guilt, blame or regrets or the betrayal she felt.

God help her.

What she saw in her hero's eyes, in the hard angle of his strong jaw, was evidence of deep, abiding love for his wife. All she had ever wanted for herself. Proof of what she had sacrificed everything for. Testament to the heart's desire she would take to a lonely grave with the epitaph *Should have known better.*

All she wanted was a man who loved her as much as this man had loved his wife.

The should-have-known-better part of her wanted to stand back and debunk the evidence of true love for a lie. She was beyond tipsy, unguarded really. Vulnerable. His tears might be real, but she might be mistaken. Maybe he'd cheated on his wife. Maybe he hadn't really loved her at all and felt really rotten about that.

The beat of the music pounded up through the floor, through her feet and legs. Her body thrummed. Her judgment seemed on permanent holiday, but she knew the should-have-known-better part of her couldn't even begin to comprehend a real hero.

She had no illusions left to shatter.

He danced with her awhile, the slow, steamy riffs. Her hand fit wholly in his. He drank more Wild Turkey, then switched to brandy with her.

She had the impression the woman he buried that afternoon was only the last in a string of burials, of devastating losses, but he wouldn't elaborate.

She understood why. Accidents happen, people die, people you love so much your heart will never quieten, people you grew up with, people you only knew a few years but came to love.

Losing the woman he loved and expected to love forever was not the final blow, but the surest.

She understood through her overwarm, clouded thoughts that some crucial juncture was met and then passed between them. What happened in those hours happened out of time and space, beyond reality, into a cocoon where his incomprehensible loss could be assuaged, and her overpowering loneliness defeated, if only for the moment.

She needed what she had never known. He needed what he would never know again.

She learned his dead wife's name, never his. Nor was there ever a moment, Kirsten knew, when it wasn't Margo on his mind, Margo in his mind's eye, Margo in his heart.

Or, eventually, Margo in his arms, the one to whom he made such a tender, aching farewell in Kirsten's bed.

But she could pretend, and she did. She had based her life and her judgment on the relevant facts for so long, only to learn what a lie a fact could be. So, if for one night, one precious scrap of fantasy could salvage her heart, then she would abandon the facts, and indulge, embrace the fantasy that she was loved.

On that long-ago night, Kirsten McCourt stole into the role of a woman who was well and truly loved, and she had no regrets. Ever after, she would know what that was, and what it wasn't. Even if ever after never came again.

Chapter One

Five years later

It wasn't the loincloth that got to them, but the rabbit skin decorating a loincloth over pajama bottoms, the naked chest of a four-year-old and a real medicine bag filled with treasures to ward off evil spirits.

Kirsten's son, Christo, the fiercest Indian in the Pacific Northwest came whooping, hurtling down the narrow staircase from his perch on the stair landing. It was all any of them could do to smother smiles and assume the necessary awe.

Her best friend, Ginny Wilder, on the eve of moving to a house she and her husband had already prepared near the Wyoming-Montana border, sat on the creaking old hardwood floor in Kirsten's Victorian house. Setting aside her pie plate in the nick of time, she opened her arms and Christo flew into her ample, earth-mother body.

"So Christo-man, is there anything new inside your medicine bag? Would it be okay if I peek inside?"

"Christo-man," he intoned, infusing his name

with the awesome authority of a cartoon superhero. Anything for his Aunt Ginny, who wasn't his aunt, but closer, Kirsten thought. Sure enough, Christo limited the exposure. "Just only you can see. Be careful not to spill anything."

Burton Rawlings feigned mortal injury over being left out. An old colleague of Lane's, his best friend, and every bit as much betrayed as Kirsten had been, Burton had shown up uninvited, out of the blue. If he knew he'd intruded on a very special evening, he was either insensitive enough not to care, or else hell-bent determined not to leave until Kirsten heard what he'd come to say.

Ginny's husband, Sam, a lumberjack-looking accountant, threw a fit at being excluded from viewing the contents of the medicine bag. Kirsten and Ginny shared a knowing look, for the act was little more than a ploy to get outside for a cigarette.

Christo darted after Sam, but Ginny snagged him by the jammie bottoms and dragged him into her lap. "Come here, you, and show me what you've got."

Christo put on a moue, echoing her tone and inflection perfectly. "Come here, you, an' show me what you've got."

"This kid's eerie," Burton said.

Not even looking up, as if by rote echo, Christo copied Burton's words. "This kid's eerie." But then he plucked out a piece of mica for Ginny to admire.

Looking thin and unhealthy, Burton asked, "Where'd he learn to do that?"

Kirsten laughed softly. "Television, I suppose."

"This is more than mindlessly babbling a commercial ditty."

"You've always had a knack for voices, haven't you, Christo-man?" Ginny put in. Around her, no one talked for long about a child as if they weren't even in the room.

His sly little grin told Kirsten that Christo knew he was being admired. He settled in and began pulling apart the drawstring closure of the medicine bag. "Now...where *is* that lucky charm?"

"What is this lucky-charm business?" Burton teased. "Like cereal? That's all you've got in there?"

"No way," Christo dismissed Burton's bait, bringing his little fist out of the bag. "This is a *real* charm. See?" He opened his hand. "Isn't it a real charm, Aunt Ginny?"

"Wow, yeah!" Ginny looked over Christo's head to Kirsten. "That's a real charm for sure."

Kirsten leaned forward. "If that's what I think it is, Christo, you are in deep doo-doo."

"But I *need* it, Mom." The tendons in his small neck strained. "You let me keep the feather—"

"You can always find another feather, Christo."

"No, I can't." His little jaw jutted defiantly. "Not one with spirit medicine."

"This isn't about the feather, Christo."

Obviously sensing a pitched battle, Burton made a beeline for the sideboard, poured himself some more wine and joined Sam out on the front stoop.

Ginny cradled Christo's sturdy, angry little body. A nickel-size bronze medallion, of an age to have a dark patina, hung from a delicate chain through

Ginny's fingers. Meeting Kirsten's eyes with interest in her own, she said, "Maybe for just tonight your mom will let you keep the charm in your medicine bag?"

Kirsten felt thwarted, manipulated. "I told Christo—"

"And then, I bet," Ginny went ahead, "the medicine will rub off on all your stuff so you could give the charm back?"

"Maybe." Christo accepted as solemn truth anything Ginny told him. Kirsten may have painted the night stars onto his ceiling, a campfire on the wall and mountains in the distance, but Ginny was the one, after all, who had totally disguised the offensive safety rails of Christo's brand-new child bed by making them into supports for a teepee. And then dubbed the equally noxious child monitor a magical translator of smoke signals from afar.

"I think so," Ginny affirmed. "If it's very powerful medicine, that happens sometimes. Is it very powerful?"

"It's my daddy's," Christo said.

"Really? Your daddy's?" Ginny looked to Kirsten again. "What do you think, Mommy? For tonight?"

Kirsten nodded. What else was there to do? Ginny had no kids, would never have any of her own. Sam was sterile. But Ginny had a way about her with kids, a naturalness, heart, an instinct for the shape and form of compromise that Kirsten envied fiercely. Now, though, there was a cat out of the bag Kirsten had never intended to set free. "All right. For tonight."

He stuffed the charm back into the bag before she could change her mind, then scampered up the stairs with a whoop.

Kirsten began picking up the dessert plates. Ginny followed her into the kitchen with the remains of the cherry pie and a couple of emptied glasses.

Kirsten busied herself filling the sink with soapy water. Her best friend was moving a thousand miles away, but Kirsten could think of nothing to say. The subject of Christo's new charm was hanging in the air, thicker than the scent of winter nights that came wafting in through the window cracked open over the kitchen sink.

Ginny could run a powerful waiting game. They had known each other less than four years, dating back to Kirsten's hire at the high-school academy, where Ginny was the principal, but a lot of water had passed under the bridge. A few tears, too. She picked up a tea towel and began drying glasses.

Kirsten sighed, latching on to the first topic to come to mind. ''I wish Burton hadn't shown up just as we were sitting down to eat. He's been calling lately. He thinks I have a chance of getting my old job back if we could just prove Chet Loehman is a killer, but—''

''Kirsten, stop.'' Ginny knew Kirsten's history, knew she wanted no part of her old job, and understood that whatever it was Burton Rawlings wanted stood no chance with Kirsten. Ginny wasn't willing to let her stray even a little while. ''I want to know how come I've been under the impression that Christo's was a virgin birth?''

''I never said that, Ginny.''

"You never said anything about Christo's father, period. All this time, not a word. Not to mention that there was some keepsake of the liaison—aside from Christo, anyway."

"The charm wasn't a keepsake."

"Neither is Christo. He's a living, breathing boy."

"Let's not start this, Ginny, please." She shoved the faucet arm on all the way to hot, nearly scalding herself rinsing dishes. "I won't argue that it would be lovely if Christo had a father, but he doesn't. He's too little anyway. I should never even have shown the charm to him."

"Well, that just begs the question, Kirsten. The charm—"

"The charm just got left behind, okay? I was drinking, lacking in judgment and I had mad, passionate, anonymous sex with a total stranger. That doesn't make a father out of him."

"You must have gotten a name—"

"I didn't ask. He didn't tell. All I knew was that he had what you have, Ginny. What you and Sam have. The kind of love that only happens once. In *his* case, she died. If you want to know, he buried his wife the day I buried Lane. So sue me." She was beyond tears over it, way beyond, but a hot prickling went on behind her eyes just the same. Facts were what they were, and fantasy was what it was. "I stole that woman's swan song with her husband, and I'm not sorry."

"What if someday you happened to meet up with Christo's father? What will you say?"

"Nothing."

"But Christo is his son—"

"No." She felt so fiercely unbending. "There is no baby but mine." Her heart had long since hardened to any other possibility. "I won't set Christo up with promises I can't keep about a man I don't know, who doesn't know us, who couldn't possibly want—"

"How do you know that?" Sam put in from the doorway. Kirsten spun around, not thinking to dry her hands.

"You could look for him, you know. Ask him." Sam shrugged. "Sorry, but we, um…I couldn't help overhearing. And we all could agree it isn't my tact that keeps us friends."

"Sam, don't," Ginny warned, but a look passed between them, a caress, part comfort, part understanding, altogether so intimate it ripped Kirsten's breath away.

"I have to say this, Gins. You know I have to say this." He turned his gaze on Kirsten again. "All's I'm saying, Kirsten," he went on in his quietly unemotional manner, "and this has been comin' for a long time because I think we all knew you were never going to go off and get pregnant and have a baby by yourself on purpose—it's possible this man didn't intend to go droppin' his seed without a care, any more than you intended to get pregnant."

His chin wagged, betraying more feelings than she'd ever seen Sam display. "I'd give my right arm for a kid like that. You know it's true. So if you could find Christo's father and you don't even try, the fact you didn't is going to be a logjam between you an' me for a real long time."

Standing there, Kirsten died a little inside. In some ways she was even closer to Sam than to Ginny. He had spent many hours with her. He knew her. He loved her, like a brother does a little sister. This was not the first time he had ever called her on a choice or comment or attitude he didn't approve of.

She would not stand here and pretend that she feared Christo would be rejected if ever she found his father. What she feared was that *she* would be rejected. The man who had made love to her the night Christo was conceived, even if he loved Christo, even if he turned out to be the greatest father ever, would never love her, or any woman, the way he had loved his wife.

And having once experienced it, even having stolen those hours from a dead woman, Kirsten could never settle for less than a man who loved her like that.

What Sam saw was how stricken she was, not the selfish motives themselves. He crossed the room and took her by the arms. She was struck by the glittering light in his eyes. Her throat tightened.

"You just think about it, Kirs. You know if you ever need anything, Ginny and I'll be here."

But in another half hour they were gone, and she needed them, so where was the truth in Sam's promise? She would never have been ready for them to go.

She turned to go back into the house. The silence outside would never stop unnerving her, the dearth of insects, the lack of crickets to give the night some sound. The neighborhood was a quiet one without many kids who would be out after dark either. Still, she felt an uncharacteristic wariness crawling up her spine. Burton Rawlings was standing on the stoop beneath the yellow porch light, his baseball cap clutched between his hands.

"Look, Kirsten. I know you've got a lot on your mind, but I have to talk to you. Just a minute?"

She dropped her hands into the pockets of her denim dress and nodded. Burton followed her inside. She closed the solid six-panel door behind her.

He should know before he started that she had no interest in anything to do with rectifying what had happened to them both as a result of Lane Montgomery's treachery. "Burton, there's really nothing you can say—"

"Looks like you're doing just fine," he interrupted, acknowledging her right up front. "And from all the prints I see around here, your talent sure isn't going to waste."

"Thank you." Her house on Queen Anne Hill might be old, drafty and decrepit, but it was hers. She'd turned with a vengeance from forensic *any-thing* to filling every nook and cranny with prints she'd done of all the things that fascinated her.

"Things might be heating up, so you're better off out of it anyway."

She sank to the sofa. She should have let well enough alone, but he seemed so fragile. "Heating up, how?"

"I've found a way into Loehman's inner circle." He settled back. He had her attention, but she had the feeling he was tempering his tale now as he might not have had she agreed to consider joining him. "I was out digging up some geoducks about six months ago—"

Kirsten wrinkled her nose. Even the name of the edible Pacific clams, pronounced "gooey-ducks," put Christo in spasms of giggles. Digging them out was pretty much like pulling taffy, only something *live* out of the sand. "Tell me what happened."

"I got caught in a downpour that nearly washed out the beach road. I took shelter in a little dive where if you're interested in your own health you wouldn't want beer off the tap. Couple of guys were shooting off their mouths. It wasn't long before I learned they were joining up with Loehman. The TruthSayers are even on the Internet now." He paused, shaking his head. "They're stronger than ever. Someone's gotta get in the way of Loehman and this vigilante threat."

"Grenallo hasn't stopped looking for a way to do that, Burt—"

"I'll never understand why they didn't just press on with the case they had. Sure your photographic evidence was destroyed, but you took the pictures! You were an eyewitness to the murder Loehman committed—"

"Not exactly, Burt." In her mind's eye she could recall perfectly the videographic images of a man of Loehman's height and build wearing a blue flannel shirt with a fray at the elbow on the verge of becoming a three-corner tear. At the end of the arm was a hand holding an unregistered machine pistol and at the end of that was another man's head, a young rancher who'd defied Loehman, and at the end of that split second, the man was dead of a bullet hole in the side of his head.

She'd torn through every image she had ever caught on film of Chet Loehman, and in three of them, on another occasion days earlier, he'd been wearing that shirt. The fray matched, thread for thread, and with that, her evidence and testimony was enough to convict Loehman. But she hadn't witnessed the murder herself, only caught it by the use of a remote videocam.

Burton Rawlings knew all that, but he was a geeky intellectual properties lawyer. He had no business trying to insinuate himself into a group of lawless, self-righteous vigilantes. And he didn't know how things went in a criminal trial. They could not prove by any evidence save all that was destroyed in Kirsten's lab that Loehman had ever owned a blue flannel shirt.

Grenallo made his decision. Better to wait than to have a jury return a not guilty verdict which double jeopardy would forever preclude prosecuting again.

Burton reluctantly agreed. "It's just a wonder to me Loehman didn't see fit to kill you off, too."

"He wasn't afraid of my testimony. Not without the evidence. But Lane's drowning? Loehman probably didn't even hesitate. One last warning to me, I suppose, in case Grenallo changed his mind and decided to take the case to trial after all."

"A warning?" Burton frowned. "You think... Kirsten, you think Lane's death was a warning to you?"

"Wasn't it?" Tension skittered over her nerves. She had no idea why, only a vague uneasiness.

"Never mind." His breathing changed, grew harsh. "Nothing's changed. Loehman was playing God then and he's still doing it. There's a sheriff out in Montana that busted up a couple of citizen rallies he called unlawful assembly. Now he's bought himself a space at the top of Loehman's playbill."

"Playbill," she remembered, was Loehman's name for his blacklist of those who trampled on the liberty of all citizens everywhere to exercise their constitutionally mandated rights of free speech, freedom of assembly, freedom to arm and protect themselves.

People who found their way onto Loehman's playbill suffered. Some from crippling or fatal accidents, others, from devastating lies. Lethal rumors propagated by Loehman's machine.

Burton seemed to come to some sudden decision to wind it up. "So anyway, these yahoos I met are getting leery of me. I thought of you. Who'd believe a pretty little thing like you was out to bust their chops?"

"I can't do it, Burton." The truth was, neither could he. Loehman was never going to be vulnerable to the likes of Burton Rawlings. She sensed there was more he hadn't said, but whatever it was, she didn't want to know.

"Will you do me a favor, Burt? Take care of yourself. Don't be a cowboy. I don't want to hear of anything happening to you."

"Me and my scrawny butt? Nah. I'll be fine. Nice meeting your friends. And Christo."

Burton let himself out. After he was gone, Kirsten wandered through the living room, straightening up.

Maybe it wasn't so awful that he'd been there. At least he'd managed to distract her from the pain of watching Ginny and Sam drive off. But the house was so quiet now that all she could think about was just how she and Christo would miss them.

She turned off the downstairs lights and checked on Christo. He was curled up so far inside the teepee she could only catch a glimpse of the sweet cowlick in his dark brown hair. She sat a moment on the floor beside his bed, inhaling the little-boy scents, listening to him breathe. She couldn't imagine her life without him.

Couldn't imagine her life with his father in it in any capacity. She rose, touched her fingers to her lips and transferred a kiss and a blessing to the teepee, then took a long shower.

When she'd planted herself in the middle of her bed, she could no longer avoid thinking about disappointing Sam. Or imagining all the ways she could search for Christo's father, and legitimately fail to find him. Like sea tide to the shore, she was drawn to her computer.

To the photo files and the likeness she had created from memory in the Identicomp software she had contributed to developing herself.

It wasn't that she sat in the dark of night mooning over him.

She had never had any illusions, or intended to recall what he looked like. But the day the home pregnancy test kit had confirmed Christo's existence, Kirsten sat down to re-create his father's image.

She had keyed in the commands to print the digital image when she heard a crackling noise coming from her room. She switched off the computer, then got up from her chair to check out the noise. Christo was jabbering in his sleep, but that wouldn't account for the kind of feedback she was hearing. Was it possible the baby monitor was picking up a radio transmission of some kind?

She went back and sat on the side of her bed, waiting, staring at the monitor on her nightstand. She switched off the lamp. Moonlight bathed the corner of the bed and the floor with a silvery flash of light, and in the same instant, a voice, a man's voice, came with perfect clarity through Christo's baby monitor.

"No, this can't wait." An angry, impatient man. Her eyes began to adjust to the faint moonlight slanting through the windows. There followed a long silence, then, "Well, you tell him for me that I am not taking the flak for this one."

She sat stock-still, huddled in her flannel nightgown, trying to think what kind of fluke this was. The voice sounded tough and harsh, muttering a small succession of obscenities.

Then, "No, well…" Crackling again. "…tell string of events here." She knew what she heard was jumbled, interrupted, making no sense. "He'd better order a hit now, before this little worm figures out what's going down and gets us all fried." Another pause. "Yeah, the cops have got squat for

brains. That's mostly the damned problem, isn't it?"
Static. "Y'all have yerselves a nice night, too."

Then a clicking noise of a broken connection came as clearly through the monitor as through a phone receiver.

The obscenities alone were dismaying; the content scared her, and she wasn't easily scared. This was different. Ugly. She stood, wrapping her arms around herself, clutching her shoulders, pacing. How many ways could "put out the hit" be taken? There was no other interpretation save a murder.

An assassination plot.

She couldn't pretend otherwise, or that she didn't understand, or that she wished she'd never heard anything at all. Even if she weren't the daughter of a cop, even if she hadn't done a stint in undercover hell herself, even if she hadn't taken and examined thousands of crime-scene photos, she would know what this was—and have the duty of any citizen to report the threat of violence.

This vile, creepy stuff coming through the baby monitor was not something she could ignore or wish away. Someone, some "worm" was in very grave danger.

But dear God, why her? Why now? On top of losing Sam and Ginny to the wilds of Wyoming, she didn't need this. Her head began to throb.

But as her dad, bless his black Irish soul, would say, the poor, sorry sap with the bullet in his head would gladly have traded her the headache.

But of course, ugly and dangerous as the threat was, it gave her reason enough to postpone even thinking about looking for the man who was Christo's father.

Chapter Two

Garrett Weisz had no idea how long the pager in the pocket of his Levi's had been vibrating. He'd been manhandling a jackhammer for the past thirty minutes, tearing out the concrete on a demolition project near the wharf.

His whole body felt numb. His hands ached. His teeth felt as though they'd been rattled loose, and his ears, despite the plugs, were still ringing. All this undercover fun and games for a crack at a guy Garrett had reason to believe was uniquely positioned in the new and renewed TruthSayers.

The guy, his target, was Garrett's boss on the demolition crew. Smart, tight-lipped. The kind who played his cards close to the vest, but who, deep in his heart, longed to be tight with other right-thinking men like him. The kind of secret fanatic, Garrett thought, without a shred of tolerance for anyone who didn't think exactly as he did.

He was a hairbreadth from counting Garrett into his secret vigilante club. So close Garrett could smell it. He'd made a backhanded comment about

Garrett coming along for a "meet" with the others on Wednesday night.

Shutting down the pneumatics on the jackhammer, Garrett lowered the bandanna that covered his nose and mouth. He'd downed a quart of water before he realized his pager was vibrating. He tugged off a sweaty leather glove and dug the thing out of his pocket when the boss man moved in behind him.

"That it? They find your female?"

Garrett nodded. His cover story was that he had to carry a pager because his wife had bolted and run off with his kids. For a touch of the plausible, he held up the pager so the boss man could see that it was indeed the Seattle police paging him.

"You take off, then. I'll give you the whole day's pay. You probably earned that already. Get things settled at home an' I'll see you back here in the morning." He stuck out his hand for a show of male solidarity. Disgusted, Garrett shook hands.

All in a day's work.

He walked off the job to a battered old pickup parked at the perimeter of the job site. He stuck a hand under his arm and pulled off the other glove, then hopped in, fired up and pulled out into the late-morning traffic. He flipped on the switch of a police radio that looked like an ordinary trucker's CB.

Some detective named Vorees came on within a thirty-second hold. "Weisz?"

"Yeah. Who am I talking to?"

"Ross Vorees, Division Seven Detective Squad."

"Reporting to who?"

Vorees named his chief, finally a name Garrett recognized.

"What have you got?"

"Kirsten McCourt, cooling her heels in my conference room. Name ring a bell?"

A distant one. "One of Grenallo's people, four, five years ago? The woman whose husband was murdered?"

"That'd be the one."

"Why is she there? What's happened?"

"She's reporting she overheard half of an interesting dialogue where String's name came up." He paused. "Get this. She heard it over a baby monitor."

Garrett's pulse picked up. "What the hell is a baby monitor?"

"One of those radio transmitters you put in a kid's room. Look, Weisz. I'm aware this is a political hot potato. String's name popping up in any conversation makes it your territory. But I'd like to be in on this one, and—"

"That's negotiable." He didn't quite grasp the concept of a transmitter in a kid's room, but the rest suggested to Garrett that Kirsten McCourt's house must at least be in the neighborhood of action he wanted to penetrate. More than he had wanted anything in a real long time.

Among the TruthSayers "String" was the most recent code name for Chet Loehman. The man was a murderer and worse. His malignant influence on others—inducing hate-crime tactics, inveigling fear, discouraging freethinking under the banner of real law and order—struck at roots deep in Garrett's heart and mind and history.

String's moniker alone jerked Garrett's chain. It

went with the territory that the success of an undercover cop depended absolutely upon his ability to
think the way his enemies thought. If you couldn't
do that, you couldn't begin to imagine how twisted
a mind could become, how black a heart, how ugly
the rationalizations.

Garrett knew how String thought, so he knew the
name was an allusion to stringing people along like
lemmings or lambs to the slaughter. Otherwise, people were generally too stupid to grasp the threats to
their freedom from left-wing bleeding-heart liberals
who made criminals of armed, concerned citizens
and let the real criminals go free every time.

Garrett pulled to a stop behind an RV at the in-
tersection of his turn south and forced himself to
focus on the present moment, winding up the call
with Vorees. "I'll be there in fifteen, twenty
minutes. Whatever you do, make sure the McCourt
woman doesn't walk out of there."

"Done."

His next call was to his own office. His hands
were just about recovered enough from wielding the
jackhammer for his fingers to move. He was pounding cement dust off his jeans when J. D. Thorne,
one of his undercover team, answered. He relayed
the essentials, had J.D. page Matt Guiliani, the third
member of his team, to the station house where Vorees was sitting on McCourt.

"And, J.D., have someone check out the area
where McCourt lives. See who's new to the neighborhood. Also, find out if anyone followed her to
the station house."

"What do you want, *kemo sabe?* A car-to-car

search?'' J.D. gibed. J.D. *was* a lone ranger. He'd rather have been running this undercover operation from the get-go, and it was a constant source of tension between them that the leadership had fallen to Garrett.

"Come on, Thorne," he cajoled, downshifting around a corner. "Use your imagination. I know you've got one locked up inside that prickly exterior somewhere."

Garrett skipped the fond farewells. He respected the hell out of Thorne, but they'd be butting heads till one or the other of them found a different arena.

He pulled into a gated entrance of the station house and worked his way to Vorees's desk.

Vorees looked up. "Weisz?"

Garrett didn't bother confirming. "Where's the McCourt woman?"

Vorees stood, rising to his full six-three. "This way." He led Garrett down the hall to the observation window looking in on the interview room. "The redhead," Vorees explained on the way, "is one of our detectives, Ann Calder. The other one is Kirsten McCourt."

Garrett turned the corner, glanced at the window, then through it, then began to hear his own pulse throbbing in his ears as he stared at Kirsten McCourt.

His hands felt clammy, his feet, suddenly, impossibly riveted to the floor. She wasn't what he expected, only he didn't know what it was he'd expected or why he was reacting to her as though he hadn't ever seen a woman before.

She wasn't smiling. A pretty smile was the first

thing he would have said he looked for in a woman. She wasn't happy. He wasn't attracted to unhappy women. She was pacing, but she wasn't tall with legs that went on forever. Still, he couldn't take his eyes off her, or slow his heartbeat, or move his feet or find his balance.

Vorees was watching him, he knew. He creased his forehead and pretended to study her, as if to discern her game, when in fact it was his own game he needed to make sense of. He flashed on a night years ago, another time, when he'd been so enamored of a woman he didn't even know, that he couldn't see straight.

The night of the day he'd buried Margo.

It was the same with this woman, with Kirsten McCourt. The Wild Turkey might have had something to do with it that night, with that woman.

Not now, with this woman. Unsmiling and unhappy, and still he was drawn to her. He needed to get a grip, needed a few moments to collect himself before he talked to her.

He forced himself to turn, lean a shoulder into the window and regard Vorees, acting as if he'd about summed her up. "What's your take?"

Vorees shrugged. "She's no flake-case. She thinks she's done her civic duty. She wants out of here."

"Guiliani and Thorne here?"

"In Tactical." Vorees led Garrett to a small room with maps covering all the available wall space, several fax machines, computers and printers. "It's impressive," he said, "the information they've already managed to pull together."

Garrett expected nothing less. They were a crack team, the three of them, always outdoing themselves. He never minded dealing with whatever agency or bureaucrat cried foul over their tactics.

Garrett trusted both men on his team implicitly, but he realized now how vulnerable he was. They knew him too well. They would see through him, see that something about Kirsten McCourt had gotten under his skin.

He came up between Guiliani and Thorne, who were standing over a computer monitor displaying a neighborhood map of Queen Anne Hill, six streets in both directions. "Where are we?"

Thorne tapped a pencil eraser against the screen. "McCourt's house. Utility main—here, telephone switching—here, typical neighborhood demographics, maybe a little older population than you'd expect."

"Any newcomers?" Garrett asked.

"Wouldn't you know," Thorne responded, again bouncing a pencil eraser off the screen. "Here, across the street, one house down, converted to a rental property four months ago."

"And we know that because…"

"The owners are out of state," Vorees answered. "Phone number's the same, the account name is the same, but the bills are being paid in cash. Same with gas and electric. Usage is way above what it always has been. Somebody's living there, eating up electric, and it isn't the owners."

Gratified, he nodded. He tried to reassure himself that what had happened to him at that two-way mirror hadn't happened, and then confirmed that his other requests had been handled as well. "Okay. What about McCourt? What do we know of her activities since she left the U.S. Attorney's office?"

Matt Guiliani answered. "She teaches at a private high-school academy. Has a son named Christo, four years old. Quiet life, no indication from her that she suspects anything beyond having heard an anonymous threat. She's just being your good citizen, and she isn't very happy about being kept waiting."

Vorees added, "She's never heard of String. When she repeats what she heard, she doesn't give the word the emphasis you'd give if you knew it was referring to a person."

"Where's the little kid now?" Garrett asked.

"Some day-care operation—"

Garrett looked up at Vorees, who knew before his lips clapped shut that his answer was vague and therefore useless. Vorees went to the door and bellowed for Ann Calder, the first detective to have heard Kirsten's report. Calder, Vorees informed the group, hadn't made any note of the name of the day-care center in her report.

Ann hurried in. A thin, pretty redhead, she answered crisply. "The day care is the Gingerbread House." She walked to the map and pointed out the location, roughly halfway between Kirsten's home address and the private academy.

Looking up from the faxed report of Kirsten McCourt's employment record, Garrett waited, frowning. "Can you spare someone to keep a watch on the Gingerbread House?" Garrett asked.

Calder blanched. "I didn't even think about McCourt's kid being in any danger—"

Garrett handed off the fax to J.D., who was watching Calder with a little more intensity than was strictly necessary. *Et tu?* Garrett thought.

"If he were your kid?" J.D. asked softly. Another interesting reaction.

Calder nodded. "I'd want someone there."

Garrett sighed heavily. "Me, too. Probably overkill, but better safe than sorry. I'd like someone covering Gingerbread till it closes—or we figure out how we want to handle this." He smiled, pulling out the stops. He'd get his way without leaking charm, but he preferred to leave happy campers in his wake. "Those places do close at night?"

"Most of them." Calder smiled back, reaching for a phone, her eyes lingering a second too long with J.D. "I'll take care of it right now. But if you don't get in there, you're going to lose her."

FIFTY MINUTES after they'd stashed her in the conference room, Kirsten sat down and turned her chair to face the door. She pulled out a nail file and began working on a ragged edge. She'd give them nine more, not one minute over an hour. She'd promised Christo time to feed the ducks with day-old bread from the Scratch Bakery, and she wasn't waiting beyond that.

At fifty-eight minutes she heard a rush of movement outside the door and saw through the small glass-and-wire window several men milling around.

At fifty-nine minutes she rose to go open the door herself and invite them all to have their little confab without her, but then the door opened and a man walked in, dressed in Levi's, heavy steel-toed work boots, a dusty gray canvas jacket and a black paisley bandanna.

On the hour, she sank back into her chair, clutching at its arms. The face was the same as the one on the high-tech colored graphics printer beside her computer in the small home office next to Christo's room.

His father.

SHE HAD AN IMAGE, in her heart, of her world having stopped. Just...stopped.

Time no longer ticked. The globe ceased turning. Her world would never return again to its faithful path in the heavens.

Kirsten sat looking up into the eyes of a man who didn't recognize her, didn't know her from Eve, didn't see or remember. But because of Christo, he was as intimately connected to her as it was possible for a man and woman who didn't know each other's names.

He must have introduced himself. She saw his lips move but she didn't hear anything. Could there be a roar of silence?

He frowned. She watched the furrows develop. She thought, apropos of nothing, how she'd made a couple of minor mistakes. That there was a vertical crease between his eyebrows above that compelling, sternly aquiline nose that she hadn't gotten quite right.

''Kirsten?'' He shrugged out of his canvas jacket. Beneath it was a teal and beige–colored plaid, and beneath that, a gray T-shirt where, below that, nestled in thick black chest hairs straying upward to-

ward his Adam's apple, he'd worn the antique
bronze charm Christo now coveted for his medicine
bag.

He pulled up a pant leg at the thigh and sat half
on, half off the table in the interview room, not so
near as to be threatening, near enough to be just
familiar. "It's all right if I call you Kirsten?"

She shrugged, half nodding, numb. "Fine."

"Are you all right?"

Would she ever be? She felt stupidly melodra-
matic, out of sync, out of control. "Fine."

"You don't look so fine." He was, she thought,
legitimately caring. "Have we met? Is it me?"

She had to cope, had to pull herself together. She
would have to tell him. She would tell him. Fate had
conspired to make unnecessary any search for him.
But...not now. "I...it's only that I haven't eaten, I
think."

Without looking away from her, he said, "Somebody get some decent food in here, huh?" She had
the sense of someone moving to comply. Then, to
her, softly, "I'm sorry you've had to wait. And that
I had to come in here looking like this—" He gestured at the work boots and Levi's with cement dust
ingrained. "Do you think you could tell me what
happened last night?"

She swallowed. "I've already told the others—"

"I know. I need to hear it from the beginning."

"And I have to pick up my son from day care.
We're going to feed the ducks—" She broke off.
His smile over the ducks was too tender to bear.
"Please. I've already been through this. I told De-

tective Calder everything I know, everything I heard. That's all there is!''

Christo's father looked steadily at her, as if he knew there was not only a great deal more to tell, but that she knew she was in a position to know that herself. She knew it was all her raw feelings. That there was absolutely no way he knew what she knew, or what it meant to him.

''Kirsten.''

''Yes.''

''Let me ask you this.'' He waited while one of the guys who had come in with him interrupted to put a deli-wrapped ham-and-cheese sandwich in front of her. Produced, as if by magic, at his request. ''You worked for the U.S. Attorney's office four years ago. Is that right?''

''Yes.'' But what did that have to do with anything? She took a small bit of ham out of the sandwich and ate it.

''You were assigned to the TruthSayers task force?''

''Mr....I'm sorry. I missed your name.''

''Weisz. Garrett Weisz. Your waiter today,'' he said, indicating the medium-built Latin-lover-type man who'd put the food in front of her, ''is Matt Guiliani. Guili, we call him. That's J. D. Thorne, otherwise known as the thorn in my side.'' A strong, silent type. ''You've met Detective Vorees.''

She began to recover her wits. She could, if asked, recite back their names now, even his, Christo's father's name. ''Well, Mr. Weisz, you obviously already know everything but my blood type—''

''I think that's somewhere in your employment

records, too,'' he interrupted, deadpan. But she must have looked as benumbed as she felt. ''That was supposed to be a joke. Just to lighten things up a little.''

''Yo, you're a laugh a minute, bro,'' Guiliani razzed. He looked at Kirsten and winked. ''Weisz-acre, that's what we call *him*.''

Kirsten smiled uncertainly. Confusion piled on the numbness. She had barely the time to register Christo's father sitting here cross-examining her. She didn't know what to do with Guiliani's obvious fondness for Garrett Weisz. There was a powerful bond between them.

''So.'' She breathed deeply, and focused on a point between the eyes of the father of her son. ''You know where I've been, what I've done, and none of it has anything to do with what I heard last night.''

''There's a strong possibility that you're mistaken in that, Kirsten. That's the problem. That's why Detective Vorees took the case out of the hands of Ann Calder, that's why I'm in on this thing. That's why we have to start at the beginning.''

''No...listen, really.'' An uneasiness began to congeal inside her, separate from the shock of being confronted with Christo's father. To do now with the anxiety Vorees had originally incited in her. ''This was just some weird, random thing...'' Maybe he would believe her if she said it one more time. ''If you insist, I'll give you my statement again so you can hear all the details for yourselves, but then I really need to go.''

Garrett picked up Ann Calder's notes. ''Is this a

direct quote: *'No, well...string of events here...he'd better order a hit now'*? This is accurate?''

''Yes.''

''Do you know what worm is being talked about?''

''How would I know that, Mr. Weisz? I have never—'' She broke off as Weisz lowered his head and gnawed on the inside of his lower lip. She read a steep resistance to say anything more into his body language. A sensation of panic rose inside her. Something dreadfully certain that her expectation of things going terribly wrong here had been dead-on accurate.

Christo's father looked at her again, as if he should know her, which was no comfort at all. ''Would you have an idea of the identity of the worm if I told you String is a code name, a personal handle—an alias—used by Chet Loehman?''

She felt the heat drain out of her body. ''You must be mistaken.''

''About String? I'm not.''

''I never heard that.''

''You wouldn't have. His organization has evolved, Kirsten, since you were a part of the task force.''

''That doesn't mean that 'string' in what I heard has any connection to Loehman.''

''Do you think it's a coincidence, Kirsten?'' Thorne put in from her immediate left. ''Some wildly improbable fluke, that you happened to have been number one on Loehman's playbill, and now this is going on around you?''

Loehman's playbill. Twice inside twelve hours...

Guiliani glared. "Give it a rest, Thorne. How'd you like it if somebody flapped some deadly coincidence from your past in your face?"

"What is this?" Kirsten demanded, latching on to a scrap of anger from the heap of confusion. "Some good cop, bad cop routine? What do you want from me that you're not getting?"

"Kirsten—"

She ignored Garrett's attempt to stop her. "No! Am I seriously supposed to believe that all these years later some unwitting idiot in the employ of Chet Loehman chose my house and my child's monitor to tap into and tip me off to an incriminating solicitation for murder? What sense does that make?"

Garrett rose from where he'd been sitting on the table and pulled a chair out on its casters. He sat before her and eased the angle of swivel in her chair so that they were face-to-face, knees almost as close as they had been that night beneath the booth in the Mercury Club. She couldn't escape that heat, the brush of denim, the wash of memories, the tug of attraction real and with her right now.

"Kirsten, I understand what you're saying. You've got great instincts—"

"I have lousy instincts, Mr. Weisz," she snapped. "That's why Loehman is still free. But I'm not stupid, and neither is he. I was neutralized, so far as he is concerned, years ago. So—"

Garrett Weisz held up a hand to interrupt her. "Kirsten, I know on the face of it this scenario is a reach. We all know Loehman doesn't suffer fools, and the likelihood of something like this happening to you is about fifty million to one.''

''If you know that, then play the odds, Mr. Weisz. Assume a fluke. Take the monitor. You're welcome to it.''

He shook his head. ''Kirsten, it's just not that easy.''

Chapter Three

She stared at him. "Nothing ever is, is it?"

"We're not saying," he went on, insistent but kind, "that there's any proof the 'string' in what you heard is necessarily Loehman." She could see that he believed it was, though, with every fiber in him. "All I'm asking, here, Kirsten, is for you to just open up a space in your thinking and see if something about what happened last night with the—" He broke off, looking abashed.

"Baby monitor," Ann Calder supplied.

"The baby monitor," he went on. "About all that somehow making perfect sense when you know that String is an alias that Loehman uses."

She felt herself getting a little beyond the panic. "Where were you five years ago?"

"During the first task force investigation, you mean?"

She nodded, though strobelike images deep in her memory conjured the booth in the seventies disco, the touch of his lips to her fingers, his tongue to her wrist, the brush of him against her flat belly, the desperate stolen kiss in the dark of her hotel room.

"Winding up a tour of duty in the navy." He cracked a grin. "Commonly referred to by the oxymoron 'military intelligence.'"

She smiled, tricked by the self-deprecating humor, in spite of everything. In spite of the visceral, heated memory. "That explains it."

"Whoa," Guiliani cracked. "Better watch your step, *paisan*."

"I am not your *paisan*," Garrett retorted. "Budapest has got it all over Palermo."

"Says you. Whatever. The lady's got your number."

Garrett sent a rude look at Guiliani, then turned back to Kirsten. "Don't mind the comic relief here, Kirsten. Just try to think what might make any of this make sense. Is there anything?"

She was still back on the reference to Budapest. Her baby's father was Hungarian, then. And the castle on Christo's charm, a castle that was different from any she had ever seen, must be in Budapest.

She wrenched her thoughts away from dangerous details to search for some meaning in what she had heard over the monitor. "I haven't kept up on the case at all. It's not my job or my concern anymore."

Weisz only nodded, waiting for her to go on. Did he think if she just kept talking she would devise some scenario to suit his request?

"I...I'm a teacher now."

"Really." She could tell he already knew that. "Are you missing classes right now?"

"No. I have this quarter off."

"What do you teach?"

"Graphic arts, photography, videography—at a

private high-school academy. I don't have any interest in any of this—which is exactly what I told—'' She broke off, as suddenly everything became sickeningly clear and the space Garrett Wcisz had asked for cracked open in her mind.

Burton Rawlings had been phoning her on and off for four or five months. And last night he'd been in her home for several hours, staying even after Ginny and Sam left, with Loehman's playbill on his mind.

''Kirsten?'' Garrett's voice deepened. The tension around the room grew thick enough to spread with a trowel.

Her hands fisted. She tucked each under the other arm below her breasts. If she could only get through this, maybe they would leave her alone.

''Last night I had a farewell dinner for friends of mine. Ginny and Sam Wilder. Ginny is…was the principal at the academy where I teach. An attorney I used to know from my work in John Grenallo's office stopped by. He'd been calling me. Somehow, he just…he stayed for dinner, waiting for the chance to talk privately.''

''What's his name?'' J.D. asked.

''Rawlings. Burton Rawlings.''

''What'd he want?'' Guiliani this time. Garrett sat watching her intently. Kindly.

''He said he'd run into a couple of guys that he believed are involved with Chet Loehman. He said they were getting suspicious of him, and he somehow thought I could ease the problem.''

''So, he was thinking he had an entrée of sorts to Loehman's inner circle?''

"Yes."

"And he wanted you in?"

"Yes. He assumed I would still jump at a chance to set things right with Grenallo's office. Burt had been burned, too. I don't think he'll ever get over it. But he felt bad about the way things happened when the investigation fell apart five years ago—"

"So bad, he was offering you the chance to re-deem yourself?" Guiliani demanded. "The guy must be some bricks short of a load. You've got a little kid—"

"Pipe down and let the lady talk," Garrett commanded, his voice low, strained.

She started to say something, but then shrugged. "To be fair, I don't think Burton even knew about Christo—" She broke off, swallowing hard. It felt dangerous to her even to say Christo's name in front of Garrett Weisz. "At least not before he came to the house last night. He understands now. Do you…are you thinking this guy whose voice I heard may have followed Burton to my house?"

"It's possible." Garrett leaned forward, his fore-arms on his thighs, hands dangling between them. The posture put him nearer eye-to-eye with her. She'd forgotten how tall he was, how broad his shoulders were. He seemed now to create a space around them from which the others were excluded. He met her eyes. For the first time she saw that his were not blue at all, but gray, rimmed with a deep sea-green at the outer edge of his irises. "Not very likely, though."

"Why? Doesn't it make sense that that's why the

guy was anywhere near my house when that call was made?''

''How long was it between the time that Rawlings left and you heard what you heard?''

''A while.'' Her nails combed a path through her hair, pulled back in her customary chignon. She knew exactly where this was leading, exactly where it wasn't. Burton was long gone by the time she heard anything. ''Two cars could have followed Burton to my house. Or one followed him, and another one came after, so they could follow him when he left and still leave someone behind to make sure that I didn't leave later as well.'' Her teeth clenched. ''They were following him. Not me. He won't be coming back, so there isn't a problem.''

Garrett Weisz lowered his head. She could see, though his full head of shiny coal-black hair was creased by the band of a hard hat, the same cowlick as Christo's.

He looked back up at her. ''You don't believe that, Kirsten. You know better. It's pointless—''

''I don't. You watch. One more night or two, take the baby monitor. You'll see. *They'll* see I'm not involved.''

''Are you saying, Kirsten, that Rawlings just turned up after all this time? Are you sure you hadn't heard from him, one way or another, before last night. Had he called you at all? See, if he'd called you, and his phone calls were being intercepted somehow, then—''

''I know how it works.'' Burton had called her, and it was impossible to miss the meaning or the consequence. Someone could have been watching her house since the first time, back in June or July, that Burton phoned her.

She couldn't sit there any longer. She had to leave now, go pick up Christo and drive as far away as she could get before exhaustion set in, then five hundred miles more. She stood, pulling the strap of her bag up onto her shoulder. "I have to go."

She began to dig into her purse for her keys, to hand over the keys to her house. The cold inside her now grew so severe, she burned with it. She fell to babbling, offering her keys, her house, the offending monitor, the dregs of her life. "I'm going to get Christo now, and leave." Her hands shook. It was her car key that fell from the chain.

Weisz picked it up off the carpeted floor and sat there, turning it over and over in his hands. "That was my father's name." His voice deepened, went guttural with emotion and inflection. "Kryztov."

She froze.

"I agree with you, Kirsten," he said. "Christo has to go."

"Yes. And I—" She stopped short, unable to even vocalize her understanding of what he meant by that.

He reached out to her. She could feel in his reach, see in his eyes a flicker of recognition, the whisper of attraction to her, the pull of history that hadn't yet dawned on him. "Kirsten—"

"Don't touch me!"

"Okay. Okay, Kirsten. Take it easy." His tone was both respectful and sympathetic, which only made her feel more threatened. He didn't want a battle with her, and he was trying not to cram anything down her throat. He backed off, spreading his hands as if she were aiming a gun at him. She was only vaguely aware of the others.

"Kirsten, we've already got plainclothes cops watching over Gingerbread. We have to assure Christo's safety. We can't afford to make any rash moves or take any chances. You've got to know, Christo is my first concern."

"Oh, God..." Her emotions so nearly over the top, an anguished cry escaped her throat. "Christo is *my* concern, and I'm leaving. Loehman will know when I'm gone that I'm not a threat to him. He—"

"What about other people's babies, Kirsten?" Thorne asked, his voice low, demanding, sharp. "What about that sheriff in Montana? You think he isn't toast? You think he doesn't have kids, family? What about—"

"Thorne," Garrett interrupted, glancing only momentarily away from her. "Not now, huh? In fact, everyone clear out. All of you. Just leave us alone for a minute."

He exchanged another look with Thorne, who was the last to leave. Thorne said, "There's a window overlooking the parking lot in the bureau chief's office."

"Fine." Garrett rose, ushered Thorne out and closed the door behind him.

And Kirsten was alone with Garrett Weisz for the first time in five years. She felt trapped on every level, cornered.

"Kirsten, will you sit with me for a minute? Just collect yourself and hear me out?"

"No." But she did sit. She had to draw on every

internal resource she had ever in her life called upon to keep herself together. Christo was safe, so far, if Weisz's word was worth anything. In another hour she would take Christo away from here, away from anyone who had ever even heard of Chet Loehman, even if that meant going to Greenland.

"I'm sorry," she said. "I can't help you. I'm responsible for myself and my son, and I'm not going to accept that I'm the only thing standing between Loehman's goons and that sheriff's life."

"Kirsten, listen to me." He managed to say somehow, to close in on her without warning or threat. His voice stilled her, his deep gray eyes commanded hers. He came close enough in his chair to lean forward. Cupping her icy hands in his, he drew them up till his lips touched her fingertips, and he breathed warmed air to dispel the chill. "I'm sorry. I'm staring. I can't help feeling like I should know you."

If ever there was to be a right moment to tell him, it was now, while they were alone. But she couldn't get the words to form in her mind, or to come out her lips of their own accord.

"Well." He drew a deep breath and expelled it, dismissing the issue. "Kirsten, I want to show you something so you'll know we're not exaggerating. We're not trying to scare you. Thorne didn't mean to imply you're the only thing standing between good and evil in the universe." He broke off his gaze, laughing a little, rueful. "Ask him. He'll tell you. That's his role, see, so it couldn't be yours."

She bit her lip. "I don't feel like smiling, Mr. Weisz."

"Garrett."

"Garrett, then."

"I know. The problem is very real, Kirsten, and it's your problem, and I swear by everything that's sacred that if I could take it out of your life, I would do it. I can't. We have to deal with this. I know it's hard. I know it's a lot to expect. I know they killed your husband, and Loehman isn't known for giving more than one warning. I know Christo is waiting for you. More than the sheriff and his family, right now it's *your* life I'm concerned with. Yours and your boy's."

He knew everything, but that it was *his* son waiting for a promised trip to the park. If he knew that, would it make a difference? Would he let her go? But she couldn't tell him that, just spill it out there. The words wouldn't form, so what did it matter?

"Just hang in there with me for another few minutes. Can you do that?"

"Don't patronize me, Mr. Weisz. If I don't walk out of here right now, it won't only be another few minutes, will it?"

"No. It won't. But you don't have a choice—at least, in my opinion. You have to judge for yourself. Don't believe me. Believe what you see. That's all I'm asking."

He nodded toward the door, letting her choose her own time. She grabbed her bag and went to the door. Leaning against the wall opposite, Vorees straightened and led the way. Guiliani followed; Thorne was gone. Kirsten fell into line to the bureau chief's office. The lights were not on. The blinds were lowered, but open. Looking through the slats to the parking lot below, Garrett requested binoculars, which Guiliani handed him.

Weisz gestured for Kirsten to join him at the window. "You see that white van, four rows in, about midway down?"

She looked. "Yes."

"Do you recognize it?"

"No."

"Are you sure?"

"Not...I mean, I don't know. I may have seen it or one like it." She wanted to help, or rather, to be helpful so this could all conclude and she would know what she had to do next to protect Christo and herself.

"You'll see your car, almost straight ahead of the van, two rows over." He handed her the binoculars. "Focus on the driver of the van."

She nodded slightly. "He's holding a folded piece of newspaper up against the steering wheel. It's...a crossword puzzle."

"Okay. Keep watching." He picked up the phone on the chief's desk, punched in a number. "I just called Thorne's pager. He's about to set off a radio signal that's going to trip an alarm inside that van."

Kirsten watched through the binoculars as the driver sat studying his crossword puzzle, then for no apparent reason, jerked his head up. He tossed a pencil and the folded news page aside, rolled down the window and craned his neck to look dead ahead—where there was nothing to look at, particularly, but her car.

She lowered the binoculars as the driver of the van jerked open his door and got out. He lit a cigarette and flicked the match on the pavement, always watching her car, casting an angry glance at something inside the van.

"He could be waiting for anyone."

Garrett's look was—almost—a caress of her cheek. "He could," he agreed.

A kind of cold went through her, and took hold. The kind of cold that doesn't abate, only wends deeper. Her expertise was in video technology but it didn't take genius to figure out what had just happened before her eyes.

Her car was bugged, and Thorne's transmitter had only duplicated the electronic signal that turning the key in her own ignition would trigger.

GARRETT WATCHED Kirsten McCourt dealing with the probability that neither she nor her son, Christo, had been safe in months. He believed now that he had himself back in hand. He could admit he was attracted to her. Who cared?

It happened. Now he was working to understand her. She was just an ordinary woman with extraordinary problems. That's what he told himself, but he despised the fear Loehman evoked in her. The fear had nothing to do with a flaw in her character. She'd begged John Grenallo for another chance to go up against Loehman. Not the behavior of a fearful woman, but of one who knew the dangers Loehman presented.

Clearly, motherhood had reordered her priorities. Little Christo had changed everything for her. She no longer wanted a part of any operation intended to bring Loehman to justice.

He understood, but there wasn't any other way to exploit this opening.

Sitting at the head of the conference table with Kirsten to his left and the rest of the team around the table. Garrett made the case that whatever happened, Kirsten had to remain in her house. But he was also locking horns with Guiliani and Thorne, who before today, wouldn't have been caught dead on the same side of an argument.

Both of them wanted Kirsten taken out of the picture altogether. So maybe he was wrong. Maybe he wasn't thinking straight.

She sat numb for nearly half an hour, saying nothing. Garrett couldn't tell if she was lost in her own thoughts, or listening to the three of them wrangling. Her honey-colored hair, pulled back, seemed to him to sparkle, evoking memories or...dreams he'd had but never quite remembered.

Her eyes were the color of a small medallion he'd long since misplaced. One that had belonged to his Gypsy great-great-grandmother, bronze with a patina so dark and mysterious most people would simply call it brown and be done with it.

Compared to his, her hands were childlike; his attention riveted time and again on her wrists. The delicate bone structure, the fair skin. The perfume he'd inhaled when he blew warm air over her hands. Something inside him had stirred, something deeply imbedded in his senses, something so thick with desire he could scarcely breathe.

He didn't know where it came from, or why, or why now, and he believed it must be a fluke. He rarely had such desires, and if a stray lusty thought came along, he ignored it to a quiet death. He'd cut desire off cold with Margo's death—but he could see in Thorne's eyes the speculation he'd half expected. That Garrett was over his head with the hots for Kirsten McCourt, silently questioning Garrett's motives in insisting Kirsten must stay in her house.

Of course, J.D. wouldn't be so crass as to say so in the same room with her, but they were all so committed to truth, and they understood each other well enough that Garrett knew exactly what J.D. was thinking.

"Look," J.D. argued. "We're closing in on Loehman from half a dozen different angles. You're busy with that construction superintendent. Guili's thick as thieves with that Tri-Cities splinter group. I can sit on the baby monitor until we arrange a tap. Or Vorees can do it. If anything busts loose, we'll take it from there. But I don't think—"

"An hour ago," Garrett interrupted, "you were in Kirsten's face about the sheriff in Montana."

"A couple of hours ago," J.D. retorted, "you were seeming more objective."

His jaw tightened. Whatever it was he felt for Kirsten McCourt was never going to get in the way of doing what had to be done. "You're wrong."

"Am I?"

Guiliani stuck himself in the middle of it like a fight referee separating the combatants. "Can we stick to the point here? We've got one best choice, and that's to get Kirsten and her little kid into protective custody *now*. Then out of Loehman's reach. I think it's fairly clear she wouldn't be involved again at all if it weren't for the contacts from Burton

Rawlings. He's where we should concentrate our efforts."

"That might have been true before I came here today," Kirsten interrupted softly, the only feminine voice in the room full of men. Ann Calder had gone off after any information out there on Burton Rawlings.

Garrett realized then that Kirsten had followed the whole grueling debate. His regard for her climbed another notch. "What are you thinking, Kirsten?"

"That if I'd never come here at all today, I would be safer."

"I agree." None of the other three argued the point.

"I won't ever hear from Burton again. If the people across the street from my house are watching me, it's because Loehman knew Burton was phoning me over the past few months. Now he knows Burton was there last night—but..." She broke off. "Oh, God. Burton has to be the 'worm' they want killed!" She shook her head as if, through all this trauma, she should have thought of that much sooner.

Garrett fell back in his chair. How long could she keep getting smacked in the face with another ugly realization before she came apart? "It's a lot to take in, Kirsten."

"Yes, well, I know that." She spoke now as if she was the objective observer and not the target. "The point I'm trying to make is that if I hadn't overheard that call and come here to report it, this would all have been moot. Burton wouldn't be back, and he won't call me again. Loehman is too smart to squander his resources. He would have stopped any surveillance on me very quickly.''

''That's all well and good, Kirsten,'' Vorees said, ''but you did come. What's the bottom line here?''

''It goes back to what Loehman knows,'' Garrett answered. ''Right?'' When she nodded, he went on. ''They don't know Kirsten heard that call on Christo's monitor last night. Suppose she'd never heard it, or that she was in the shower when it happened? No one's the wiser. Kirsten knows nothing, and sooner or later they figure that out. Now, though, they have to assume she is involved. They can't afford not to assume anything but the worst. So we need a plan and we need it now.''

Aware at every minute of Kirsten seated beside him, he set out his criteria so they could throw out ideas. ''One. Kirsten has to get into her car, pick up Christo and go feed the ducks as if she has no idea she's being followed. Two. Christo needs to be removed from the situation altogether—tonight. Three. Kirsten stays, so she needs twenty-four-hour-a-day protection. Four. We have to find out why Loehman wanted her watched closely enough to set up a stakeout. And we have to do all that without spooking the spooks across the street. When we know what's at stake for Loehman, we'll know how to proceed. And maybe we'll nail the bastard once and for all.''

He sat back. He was asking a lot. He knew it. ''Ideas?''

Guili was shaking his head. ''There's no way, Weisz! You think the spooks across the street are not going to notice Christo isn't there? How suspicious is that?''

"By itself, you bet," Garrett agreed. "Think big picture.''

"How about a fake-kidnapping scenario?" Vorees suggested. "It gets Christo out, keeps Kirsten at home, cops legitimately in the house for her protection. Best of all, the spooks won't know what the hell is going on, but they sure won't leave.''

"A random kidnapping?" J.D. asked. "That's not going to create suspicion?''

"Does it matter?" Garrett wondered aloud. "Vorees has got a point. They won't know if it's real or not.''

"If it's me in their shoes, Garrett," Guili argued, "it stinks to the high heavens. Whatever their agenda, they are not going to pursue it with cops swarming all over her place, finding bugs.''

"Agreed," Garrett said.

J.D. tossed his pencil on the table. "Don't forget you've then got to keep the press under wraps. And advise the FBI that the kidnapping is phony. The more people you keep apprised of what's going on…" J.D. shrugged. He didn't have to elaborate on what happened when there were too many need-to-knows in the mix. Sooner or later there was one too many, and the whole ruse collapsed. "Not to mention, where do you take Christo?''

"Nowhere," Kirsten said, leaving no quarter for other consideration. The terror in her heart for Christo was not something hot or spontaneous or ill considered, but coldly logical. Factual. Perfectly clear. Their life on Queen Anne Hill was over, and these men had no idea, none, of what she was prepared to do to safeguard her baby's life. "There is no other way than that Christo and I both just get out." She drew her purse up onto her shoulder and stood.

Weisz got up, too, and then the others. She straightened. "Make what arrangements you like, but my son is not going anywhere without me."

Chapter Four

Garrett let her walk out. The sight of her back, of her opening the door and slipping out, gave him the sensation of having been kicked where it counted. He gritted his teeth, clamped down on whatever the hell urge it was inside him that wanted to go after her.

J.D. had the frequency of the device tied into her ignition. She wasn't going anywhere they couldn't find her inside of two seconds. Loehman's tail wasn't going to lose her, either. They had the white van marked now, as well, with a device a lot more sophisticated than the one on Kirsten's car. "Tell me again everything we know about that Truth-Sayers splinter group in the Tri-Cities."

Ann Calder came back in as Guiliani rattled off the names of the key players, the politics, the power struggle, the nature of the dispute with Loehman that had sparked the existence of the splinter group in the first place. On the same page with Garrett, he asked, "So we stir the hornet's nest a little on this? Take Loehman to the wall?"

Garrett nodded and turned to Vorees. "You got some other clothes here I could borrow?"

He shrugged. "Just sweats."

"Would you mind?"

"Be my guest."

"You're going jogging," Ann said, not a question. Barely touching the wisps of auburn hair at her neck, she blinked slowly, gave a small come-hither smile, the barest suggestion of feminine wiles. "You'll need a distraction."

Thorne all but melted. Gratified by the hint of vulnerability after Thorne had seen through Garrett's own attraction to Kirsten McCourt, feeling almost sorry for the mark in the white van, Garrett nodded. "I like your style, Ann."

Clearly not unaware of the male dynamics going on around her, she tossed her hair, then snapped out a professional, "Thank you."

"You're welcome."

Guiliani rolled his eyes. "Hey Weisz-acre. Heads up." He tossed Garrett the keys to his on-the-job junker. "The dog is along for the ride today. He might come in handy with the little kid."

KIRSTEN DROVE straight to the Scratch Bakery and picked up a couple of loaves of day-old bread for the ducks. She had no idea what she was going to do when the loaves were gone, but she didn't expect Garrett Weisz would be far behind her, either.

Garrett. Her baby's father had a name she now knew.

When he caught up with her she would tell him. Then he would understand that it was his own son's life at stake. And understanding that, he would have to abandon whatever other schemes he had concocted.

She told herself she would never go home again. Not ever. That she wouldn't hand over Christo to any kidnapping scenario. That she wouldn't have any part of a plan that separated them.

Even as she told herself those things, she knew she had no options. Ten thousand miles away would not stop Loehman. Not if he believed her to be a threat to him after he'd spared her life almost five years ago. He wouldn't rest this time, until she was dead.

It took every scrap of her energy to maintain the illusion of an ordinary day passing by. Going through rote motions, she paid for and then put the two loaves of bread into a white mesh bag she always brought along to carry out her shopping.

She walked back out into sunlight filtered through the nearly constant overcast of gray skies. A part of her wanted to scream. To take on the creep in the white van parked one car behind hers on the street in the friendly old neighborhood where she would have believed herself and Christo safe if she'd ever considered a threat to their safety at all.

She hadn't.

And without Burton Rawlings involving her so unwittingly, she wouldn't still. But she'd done the right thing and only made her own situation desperate in the doing. She tossed the bread through the window, into Christo's car seat, then drove the seven blocks to Gingerbread.

Christo sat pining away at the play table, waiting

for her. The anxiety of the extra hours of waiting wreaked havoc with his lower lip. She sank to her knees and gathered him close to her. Murmuring her love, her throat closed tight. His little arms circled her neck in a fierce hug.

"You're late, Mom. Really late."

She hugged him back as tightly, as if she would never let go. "Oh...I'm sorry." Her voice wavered oddly. Tears threatened her like rain threatened every single day in Seattle. "I'll bet the ducks are still hungry. What do you think?"

He pulled away and darted out the door, hollering behind him to come on, before the ducks got tired of waiting and flew off to the 'quator for winter. He talked a mile a minute on the way.

She watched in her rearview mirror as the white van following her pulled off to the side of the road and parked, several hundred feet behind where she always left her car whenever she and Christo drove to the park. If Weisz had someone following her as well, she couldn't spot the car.

Christo unlatched the belt of his child seat and, dragging the mesh bag with the bread in it out the door with him, rolled his eyes at her for warning again to watch what he was doing.

She felt skittish and anxious. She couldn't keep from casting a glance at the white van. Or wanting Christo to come back and take her hand. But he was only doing what he'd been doing for weeks by himself, running full bore over the grass toward the duck pond.

Weeks when she hadn't the sense to be afraid for him.

Weeks when she'd been proud of him growing so bold.

She followed after him. Her heart was stuck at her throat. She'd never known this kind of jitteriness. Approaching the pond, Christo took one of the loaves and started calling out to the ducks in his sweet, high-pitched, little-boy voice.

Christo wasn't afraid when the ducks began waddling at top speed out of the pond, up the muddy bank, coming right up to him. He didn't care if his fingers got pinched and bitten with careless, greedy duckbills.

She sat on a stone bench, soaking up every "Look, Mom!" every time he pointed out distinguishing marks on this drake or that hen. Every joyous shriek. But her pleasure was blunted by keeping watch against every imaginable threat in the vicinity. The one behind her in the white van, the couple holding hands, walking along a path from the north end.

An old man strolling by, watching Christo.

A jogger throwing a Frisbee for a hound that lacked any canine finesse.

When the bread was all gone, Christo ran along the shoreline, back and forth, clapping his hands, shouting at the ducks. She didn't recognize Christo's father till the Frisbee landed more or less at her son's feet and a basset barreled into Christo.

It all happened in the space of a few heartbeats—Christo falling hard for the dog, Garrett falling hard for fearless Christo. In about two seconds, Garrett had collapsed to the ground as if he couldn't run another stride. He told Christo the pup's name, and showed the boy how he could toss and play tug-of-war with Wag.

Inside, Kirsten reeled from her inability to recognize Garrett Weisz as the jogger until he was upon them. In the navy-blue sweats, in attitude, in his stature and carriage and posture and personality, he had seemed utterly ordinary. Unrecognizable as the man she had met one night and taken to her bed, or the undercover detective who'd sat across from her, apologetic about his construction garb.

Watching Christo, smiling at the kid-and-dog antics, he asked quietly if she minded if he joined her on the bench.

She shook her head. He would in any case. She wanted to know which of the three versions of him she had seen was the real Garrett Weisz. "You look different."

Sitting beside her, he shrugged. "Stock-in-trade, Kirsten. Comes with the territory." He gave a lopsided grin. "I intended to confess to Christo right up front that it was my fault you were late, but—"

"He's already forgotten about it." Shivering, she clutched the elbows of her coat.

He looked at her with his unmistakable gray eyes, rimmed in deep-sea green. "Be nice, wouldn't it, if that's the way the rest of the world worked."

She wanted to know what he was doing, planning.

She wanted desperately to get the words out, *That's your son.* Not because he needed or deserved or had to know for all the reasons Sam had thrust at her, but to make Garrett Weisz change his mind. She couldn't be part of his undercover plot. She had a child to grow. Their child to raise.

There is no baby but mine.

How fiercely, how recently she'd uttered those words. Now she truly knew better how fearsomely empty they had been. She couldn't get them out of her mouth for Garrett Weisz to hear. What did she think? That he would snatch up their son, strip him from her, cart him off? That he would keep Christo from her forever after?

No.

But she couldn't imagine what the consequence of telling him would be, only that there must be consequences she wasn't prepared to deal with. Not now. Her only option was to buy time, which meant sending Christo away from her and out of danger. If she and Christo were ever to be truly safe again, she had to deal with that now. First. Taking Christo out of the danger zone was the best option for them all.

Garrett hadn't attempted a word of persuasion; this she was doing to herself. "What have you done so far?" she asked him.

"Vorees is hitting up a judge for a phone tap. Guiliani took the key to your back door. Ann Calder picked up your trail and followed you here, which is how I knew where to come."

She nodded. "There aren't a lot of duck ponds around, are there?" Not with all the water surrounding Seattle. Christo knew ducks fly south for the winter, like many, many birds, but there was never any threat of these waddlers abandoning their cushy pond. "Won't your meeting me here make the guy in the van nervous?"

"Calder flattened one of her tires." He smiled.

"Pulled off quite a damsel-in-distress act. The guy's tongue is hanging out of his mouth. It'll be half an hour before he comes up for air."

He looked at her again. She saw the same kind of question in his eyes now that she'd seen the first time she laid eyes on him that night in the Mercury. *Are you doing okay?*

She looked away. What else could she do?

"Kirsten?"

"Yes?" A bad taste, fear of what might happen, of Loehman, of Weisz and his kindness, pooled unremittingly in her mouth. "Did you settle on a kidnapping?"

"Should I take it you've changed your mind?"

She nodded. With Wag in hot pursuit, Christo was somersaulting over the grass. His hair was getting wet. She had to get him home soon, dried off and warm. "I can probably handle whatever camera work you need. Photo surveillance. Digital, whatever."

Weisz clasped his hands and let out a breath. She realized he'd been worried that he'd have to find some new avenue to convince her she had to stay.

"That'd be great. What I need to know now is if you have someone to send Christo to."

There was never a question in her mind it must be Ginny and Sam. Her dad was too old and too far away. She had a sister in Phoenix, but they weren't close. Christo was only vaguely aware that he had a real aunt at all. "My friends—"

"The Wilders?"

"Yes." Her throat tightened.

He pulled out a small dedicated cell phone for

which all that was required was that he turn it on. A few seconds later, he had his connection. "We're a go for Jackson Hole." He listened for only a moment, then closed up the phone and returned it to the pocket of his hooded sweatshirt.

"You know where the Wilders are?" She felt overwhelmed, somehow outdistanced, outmaneuvered.

Out of control, emotionally, and in every other sense, if she were honest. Garrett Weisz already knew that Ginny and Sam were the people she trusted most, as well as where they were and how he was going to get Christo to safety.

If he knew all that, who else knew? "Are Ginny and Sam too obvious?"

Shaking his head, he reached out to brush a strand of hair from her face. His barest touch lit fires, fired emotions that skittered wildly. Why didn't he know, why couldn't he see, how could he fail to recognize himself in Christo?

"They would be—if we tried to pull off a random kidnapping. But it looks like a ruse to get cops inside your house. I don't think there's any possibility of that with what we've got in mind."

"Which is what?"

"Still a kidnapping," he admitted, "but a different angle." The only time he took his eyes off her was to watch Christo with Wag, or to scan the park for any signs of trouble. "This is what I believe is going on, Kirsten. If we're right about all this, then Loehman has to believe you have something, or you're working with Burton Rawlings on getting something, developing something that will destroy him, one way or another.

"Not just something nebulous, either," he went on. "Loehman is worried, but that's how the paranoid survive. He must have it reliably that you—or Burton—have solid evidence. We don't know what that is yet, which is the point of all of this."

"I don't understand… About Ginny and Sam—"

"You will. Here's the kicker. We all know you aren't Loehman's only problem. There's unrest in the troops, a lot of jockeying going on—"

"Burton said that. Too many wannabe leaders, not enough followers."

"Exactly." Wag had begun to lose interest. Garrett called to Christo and held out a handful of doggie treats, which did the trick for restoring Wag's willingness to roll over and play dead, over and over again. Christo was sneaking looks at Garrett that made him smile, and wrenched Kirsten's heart.

She tried to stay focused, summing up. "So, whatever it is Loehman thinks I've got, or that I'm going to get, is equally dangerous to him if it falls into the hands of these splinter groups?"

Garrett nodded. "You got it. Whatever hurts Loehman, whatever loosens his grip on the reins works for any of them. Maybe more for them than for us. But it wouldn't hurt my feelings to identify and nail Loehman's competition at the same time."

She swallowed. Christo fell into a giggling fit again while Wag gnawed on his fingers. She tried to think what Loehman would do, backed into a corner, not only his control threatened, but his freedom, and possibly his life. "So the kidnapping is made to look like the work of one of the factions against Loehman?''

''Yeah.''

''How will it work?''

''We'll take Christo out right after ten o'clock tonight. I have a Learjet standing by. We'll fly to Missoula and drive to the Wilders'. Christo will be snug in bed by around 2:00 a.m. I'll be back by dawn.''

She had to grit her teeth to keep from falling apart at the reality of it all happening, of Christo being taken from her, of Garrett taking Christo himself. ''Do Sam and Ginny already know—''

''They're probably hearing about it right now. Are you concerned that there'll be a problem?''

''No. None.''

He nodded. His look told her how fortunate she was to have someone to whom she could entrust Christo. Friends who could do that for her without question.

Christo came running to get help with tying a shoelace. Garrett made some appreciative noise about the outstanding sneakers. The two of them exchanged a high-five and he watched Christo take off again. ''Any doubt that Christo will be okay?''

''To wake up at Ginny and Sam's?'' Christo would be over the moon with excitement. There was no other way she could have considered any of this if she hadn't known absolutely that much was true. ''He'll be fine. I have some baby Benadryl. He's allergic to strawberries, so…''

Why was it so hard?

Why, if she could share these small details with

Garrett Weisz, was it so impossible to simply say what she knew would finally have to be said?

Every moment that slipped away added to the weight of her guilt, to the seriousness of her offense. "He sleeps well anyway. The Benadryl will ensure he doesn't wake up during the trip." She forced a smile against the glaze of tears. "If he knew he'd missed his first ride on a jet plane, hell wouldn't have him."

"I'd be the same way." Another variation on the Weisz smile, one so like Christo's grin she had to look away to breathe. "He has a temper, huh?"

If he knew he was Christo's father, could his question have sounded more chip-off-the-old-block prideful? She didn't think so. How much deeper a hole could she dig for herself?

When she didn't answer, he went back to filling her in on the rest of what would happen after Christo was gone. "We know they either have bugs planted inside your house, or some fairly sophisticated parabolic mikes. We're the enemy, so far as you're concerned. You shouldn't even think of it as an act, Kirsten."

She bowed her head a moment.

"The more violent and devastated and hysterical you manage to come across over those listening devices, the better. You're a hostage to lunatics who've just ripped your child out of your arms." He gave a half smile, a bittersweet incarnation of a smile she hadn't seen yet. "Can you do it?"

She heard only concern for her, no real doubt in his question. She nodded.

"For what it's worth, Kirsten, Christo will be

long gone, so he doesn't have to hear any of that."
He looked at her, seeming to look inside her, again
as if he should know her.

The look finally ebbed; the creases in his forehead
eased. "Anyway. You'll be made to understand that
we intend to hold Christo hostage until you hand
over to us whatever it is you've got on Loehman.
When you do, you'll get Christo back, everybody
lives happily ever after. Meanwhile, Loehman can't
afford to wait this out with surveillance trying to
figure out what you and Rawlings are up to. His
back will be up against a wall. He will have to do
something to force Rawlings's hand now."

"And when he does?"

"We'll be there. I promise you, I'll do everything
in my power." He let a shoulder rise and fall. A
shoulder she'd once seen bared, once clung to, once
clutched in the heat of the sexual release that made
it possible for her to endure the loneliness, the night.

Her darkest night.

The same act in which Christo had been conceived.

"Chances are," he offered, "no real action will
ever come close to you. The thing is, we won't know
that until we know what it is that's already got Loehman nervous enough to be monitoring your house.
Everything you do. Everywhere you go." He
watched Christo playing tug-of-war with Wag over
the Frisbee. "From now on, one of us will be with
you twenty-four-seven."

Her hands fluttered. Her nerve, so numbed now
for all these hours, began to flag. "Will Guiliani still
be at my place when Christo and I get back?"

"Is that a problem?"

"Only that I have to tell Christo something. Otherwise he'll be full of questions, jabbering his head off. He will anyway, but if they're listening—"

"Yeah." He exhaled sharply, considering. One thing out of the ordinary, even a little thing, might be enough to tip off whoever was at the other end of the listening devices in her house. Guili had to get out. They'd have to maintain their own surveillance from behind the house for at least the next several hours.

He stood. Christo came charging back and took his hand. "Can you an' Wag come over to our house?" He looked to Kirsten. "Can he, Mom?"

"Christo! What are you—" Her small lecture died in her throat. She'd just spent the last half hour talking to Garrett Weisz. What was she thinking, how could she possibly expect Christo to treat him as a stranger to be avoided?

Watching her reaction, Garrett dropped to one knee. Christo fit as naturally there as he had in Ginny's lap, as he would in Kirsten's own embrace. Garrett appeared to be less at ease. "You like Wag, huh?"

Christo pulled a well-duh look. "Can he come over, Mom? It would be just for tonight."

"Wag can't come right now, Christo," his unwitting father answered. "But you'll get to see him again. That's a promise."

"An' do you keep promises, mister?" Christo demanded.

Garrett picked up Christo's hand, and with it, crossed his own heart.

Kirsten sent Christo off to collect the trash. Garrett stood again, and she got up, intending to tell him he had no business making promises to Christo.

Before she could say anything, Garrett cut her off. ''The dog is Guiliani's. Wag is going to go with Christo.''

Tears sprang instantly to her eyes. The kindness unraveled her more efficiently than any threat or danger or intimidation would ever accomplish. ''That's not necessary, really—''

''Don't.''

She thought for one wildly confused instant that he was going to scold her, to say he would do anything for his son, Wag being the least of it…but it was to her he was so attuned, so focused. He searched her face, but then his hungry gaze settled, fixing on her lips. His own lips parted.

Her heart began to pound. She saw from the corner of her eye his hand approaching her shoulder, but then instead it was her face, then his fingers drawing aside the strands of her hair blowing around on currents of air.

Ducks quacked and geese honked overhead, Wag barked and Christo giggled and hollered delight, but what she heard was her own breath, arresting because her baby's father was touching her like a man who loved his woman.

She stood transfixed by his fingers cradling her nape, his thumb tracing the shape of her lower lip. Her own hand came naturally up to touch his wrist, but then his look, for long seconds more so achingly tender she thought she would die, darkened.

She broke off and let her hand fall away.

He stared at the ground.

She started to say his name, and broke off again.

He shoved his hands into the pockets of his sweat-shirt. There was no hint of a battle being waged inside him, but she knew, somehow.

When he spoke, it was as if he had read her mind. "Don't make the mistake of confusing me with a soft touch, Kirsten." In his eyes she found a cold, dangerous wealth of warning, another person. He was an undercover cop, a man with his own agenda and he would do what was expedient to his purposes. Nothing less.

Nor anything more.

He pulled up his hood and whistled for Wag. "On your way back to the car, remind Christo it isn't safe to talk to strangers."

Chapter Five

Missing his usual rambunctious reunion with Wag the dog, Matt Guiliani departed the lot of the downtown Seattle police station and drove to the nearest Pacific Gas & Electric substation where he signed off on the necessary paperwork and co-opted a service truck.

Whistling softly, thinking with his typical lightning speed, moving to create exactly the opposite illusion, he transferred a bunch of contraband electronic equipment from the trunk of the beat-up old Dodge to the bed of a pickup.

By the time he arrived on Kirsten McCourt's street on Queen Anne Hill, the power to the houses opposite her, where they suspected the watchers were operating, was going to go mysteriously dead.

He wanted a look inside that house before he started setting up at Kirsten's place. A lot of sheer speculation had gone into their planning and preparation. He needed to confirm for the record, for their operation, and for purposes of getting the emergency wiretap order, that the house was being used as a stakeout.

He parked on the street in front of the tall, narrow house opposite hers, threw on a tool belt and wandered south one narrow lot, then up stairs.

Drapes blocked the front windows, shades the windows of the upper floors. He'd have preferred to see the telltale glint of a high-powered telescope poking through, but no such luck.

He rang the bell, then banged on the front door when that brought no one, identifying himself as an employee of Pacific G&E.

A lot of shuffling around happened before an unshaven guy dressed in a black T-shirt and jeans opened the door, already moaning about the blankety-blank service. Matt pasted on his unflappable expression and bulled his way inside. Another guy tossed down a newspaper and headed upstairs.

Matt watched him go. "Anyway, whole doggone street's got no juice. I've got it narrowed down to a circuit somewhere inside this house." Safe bet. Amidst half a dozen pizza boxes, the refuse of several Chinese take-out meals and empty beer cans, several heavy-duty extension cords lay hastily kicked under tables. "Looks to me you're puttin' more demand on the breakers than they can handle."

One leg of a tripod stuck out a closet door—whether it boosted a camera or telescope he couldn't tell. And a box beneath the coffee table strewn with ashtrays and old coffee cups contained a small arsenal of cell phones.

He had enough. What he'd already seen in this house met the threshold for obtaining a tap. All he had to do was send a silent signal from his pager to the attorneys standing by outside Judge Schumann's chambers, but he held off. Patience was, he'd found, inevitably rewarded.

He made his way toward the back of the house where his reward came sooner than later. On the kitchen table half buried beneath newspapers, Matt spotted a very interesting beige metal box. A phone line was plugged into it, which could only mean one thing. The calls in were being descrambled, the calls out, scrambled.

A routine wiretap executed by the phone company was going to be of no use at all. Instead, Matt would have to tap into the calls at the point of coding technology.

Always one more wrinkle, he thought. One more escape hatch, loophole or vulnerability in the system to be exploited. Crooks were always going to find a way around the technology designed to catch them, always one step ahead. They just didn't know who they were dealing with. Yet.

On his way through the house, he'd already planted a couple of bugs himself. His own design. He thumped the metal box. "You running some kinda illicit phone operation here? 'Cuz I'm obligated to report what I see—"

"Hold on." T-shirt pulled out a business-use permit for the house address.

Matt looked at the permit. "All fresh an' new, huh? Audio engineers. Boys in the band." He was annoyed with himself that he hadn't thought of pulling business permits earlier.

He let it go. No harm, no foul.

Turning the corner by the back door, he loped

down the cellar stairs to the ancient breaker box. T-shirt followed close behind. Matt reset switches that didn't need resetting and frowned when that didn't work.

When his increasingly agitated host trudged back up the stairs, he pulled out a credit-card-size receiver-transmitter, which he thought of as the equivalent of a magic decoder ring, that tuned into frequencies much as any television or CD remote control would do.

By the time he was finished, he'd locked onto the precise radio frequency that transmitted unscrambled dialogue from the kitchen table descrambling device to the stash of cell phones in the box upstairs. Short-range, powerfully protected, carefully calibrated—it was unlikely in the extreme that signals passing between the descrambler and the cell phones could be picked up without a similarly calibrated cell phone. Now they would have one, too. A block party.

Matt grinned to himself. The boys in the band could not be faulted for their care. They'd been busted by a baby monitor.

Who knew?

It took him half an hour to leave the utility-company truck parked beside a fast-food stand and then hike back up to Kirsten McCourt's yard. She had a back door and a gated, chain-link fence thick with vines, impossible to open. When they took Christo out, it would be through the back door where the boys in the band had no surveillance capability, over the fence and back out onto the streets.

He let himself in the back door with the key Kirsten had given them and moved soundlessly through the house. A veteran of more stakeouts than he cared to remember, he gauged the angle in Kirsten's house and the viewpoint from the front window to the house across the street. The so-called audio engineers had a clean view of the north side of the living room.

Based on what he'd seen, he knew that the spooks were only interested in watching who came and went from Kirsten McCourt's house, and what was said.

He scoped out the upstairs as well.

Christo's room, with the teepee and the murals, stopped him short. It was incredible. He found himself liking Kirsten a lot.

In the room that held her computer, which from this moment would be Command Central, he plugged in his favorite toy—not counting the magic-decoder-ring device. This one created a sound barrier, a kind of white noise that rendered bugs useless, giving them one room in the house for conversations they didn't want overheard.

As much to satisfy his curiosity as anything, he swept the room as he had all the others, and located the neat round disk of a bug concealed on the back of Kirsten's high-tech printer.

He left the bug in place. Almost as an afterthought, he picked up the single sheet of paper from her printer.

His heartbeat slowed. His thoughts sped. He stood there and stared at the picture-perfect image of Garrett Weisz for a good thirty seconds, raking through and discarding explanations, one after another after another.

When no marginally valid excuse remained for the photo of an undercover cop she'd supposedly never met to be sitting on Kirsten McCourt's printer, Matt had to wonder if he might not have to rethink liking her so much.

ALL THE WAY to the car, Kirsten played out the warning to Christo.

The advice wasn't idle; she suspected Garrett Weisz was not a man of idle gestures or warnings. Even before she and Christo had started back across the lawn, she saw Ann Calder driving off, which left the guy from the white van watching her every move again.

How could she have failed to notice anyone following her for so long?

Maybe they didn't always use the van. Maybe they hadn't always followed her every move. Still, it wouldn't hurt her facade of ignorance if, as they passed within earshot, she put on a show of warning Christo against strangers.

"Especially strangers with nice dogs, Christo," she said, holding his hand on the walk to the car. She watched his little face darkening, too, and though it wasn't anything she hadn't seen before in her son, she saw now the stunning resemblance to Garrett Weisz.

To his father.

"But you—" Christo stopped midsentence, looking confused.

It wasn't fair, when she'd obviously spoken at

length with the stranger, and Christo wasn't having it. But before he could put his resentment into words of his own, she warned him again in a voice he knew better than to dispute. "Not another word, Christo. Not until we get into the car."

Safely inside the car, he started in. She apologized. "You're right, Christo. It isn't fair. I was there doing a lot of talking myself. But just in case I'm not around, you have to remember—"

"Okay, Mom. But how'm I going to see Wag again? And how come—"

"Christo, you will. You just will," she interrupted as she pulled into traffic and drove home. She had to get him off the subject. "It'll be like a birthday wish when you blow out the candles—"

"An' you can't tell anyone what you wished for or it won't come true?" His eyes lit up. "Like that?"

"Right." She pulled into her driveway. "From right now, it has to be a special secret and we won't say a word, or it won't come true."

"Well, the house doesn't 'xactly have ears, ya know."

"And your ears, little monster-mash," she said, turning toward him in a mock threat, "are going to be pinned back really tight really, really soon!"

His hair was soaked from somersaulting all over the place with Wag the dog, plastered against his skull. He fell into more fits of little-boy giggles. If anything happened to him, her heart would wither and die.

The hours left seemed at once to crawl by, and vanish into thin air. Christo was used to entertaining himself between the time they usually came home from his day care, and dinner.

Today, after a warm bath spent drawing on the wall with soapy bath crayons, he headed for the TV.

"Christo-man, don't you want to read with Mommy instead?"

"Nope. I read all day." He flipped through the channels to his shows, already an expert with the remote. "You *were* late, ya know."

"Well, then sit with me at least?" But he was in no mood to cuddle. She felt empty, unable to hold him. Incapable of sitting there listening to the *Rugrats,* she decided to just confront head-on packing clothes he would need at Ginny and Sam's. "I'm heading upstairs, then, to put away laundry and stuff."

Glued to the television, Christo was only half listening, but he thought of a question. "Can that doggy in the—" But just then he broke off, clapping a hand over his mouth, remembering about keeping the secret like birthday wishes.

For an instant more she held a forefinger to her lips, then covered Christo's verbal tracks, repeating the tune the boy had heard on "Nick-at-Night." "'How much is that doggy in the window?'" She sang the words for him, cupping her hands as though they were telling secrets. "'The one with the waggly tail.' That one? We'll sing it again later, okay?"

"'Kay." He gave her a wink.

She fled upstairs to his room. Taking out a duffel bag from his closet, she put in a stack of underpants and another of undershirts. Jeans, socks, shirts, sweatshirts. Mittens. His brand-new winter parka.

Her head ached with unspent tears. She dragged a knuckle hard over her forehead, willing the headache away, and took the duffel bag to her own closet where Christo wouldn't see it.

She went downstairs to mix up a thick warm dough so that when the shows he was allowed to watch were over she could coax him into the kitchen with her. Getting flour over everything, a good dusting on his tiny freckled nose and his hair, too, he stood over the counter on a kitchen chair, mashing the cookie cutter into the dough, cutting dumplings.

She'd microwaved a quart of frozen chicken stock, and had the pot boiling and ready by the time it grew dark outside. She let Christo spoon all the dumplings into the pot—a big concession that earned her a kiss on the cheek.

"How come you're bein' so nice, Mom?"

A shiver went through her like wind cutting through the channels. "What? The dumplings? Making you do all the work?" she scoffed. "In your dreams."

"No, in yours!" he chortled. "Can we make pudding, too?"

"We don't have any chocolate kind."

"Wullll, butterscotch is okay."

"You'll have to stir," she warned. "No quitting halfway through."

"But you'll take a turn, won't you, Mom?" He rolled his eyes. "Just if my arm gets tired anyway."

His voice was so indelibly expressive. So up and down, all around. "That's it for treats, then."

Time flew by her so quickly that before she knew it, the chicken and dumplings were all gone, there was a serious dent in the pudding into which she'd put the dose of baby Benadryl, and Christo was volunteering for bed.

She knew what was coming. He wanted the medallion back into his medicine bag, and there was no question that she'd let him have it, but she teased, "How come you're being so nice, Christo-man?"

He gave her the flirty, sidelong look she loved most of all. Grabbing up his medicine bag, he darted ahead of her to her room, yanked open the drawer and only then waited for her to open her box to get his lucky charm. He'd painted that simple balsawood box at preschool, decorating it for her with a rainbow made of starfish, so it needed something very special to go inside it. Which was how she'd come to show him the antique charm in the first place.

She thought for an instant of the vagaries in life, the off chances, the small, seemingly inconsequential acts that became life-changing events. If she'd gone to her room instead of the Mercury that night, or if Garrett Weisz had not been there, if he'd gone drinking with buddies from naval intelligence or family, or if she'd simply refused when he'd asked if she minded if he sat with her awhile...

She wouldn't have this precious, challenging, maddening, incredibly active little boy. A boy who tried so hard to be satisfied with a relic that once belonged to a real daddy.

An edgy voice issued warnings that if Garrett somehow happened to see that medallion, he would know. If despite the Benadryl, Christo woke up and went for the medallion, or if it somehow spilled out, or if Garrett indulged idle interest in what a small boy put in a medicine bag...then the problem of telling him would be solved, wouldn't it?

She didn't believe it would happen, and Christo would need the scrap of security the medallion represented.

He gave her an extra-long hug, and let her hold him for quite a while, sitting there on her bed. Her heart thumped painfully.

Another hour. Sixty more minutes before she handed Christo over to his father.

Tears congealed inside her.

She wouldn't cry, wouldn't give in to emotions over a changing reality she had no power to control. Just one more hour. She thought she would never be able to do this, then made herself buck up and follow Christo back into his room.

She dropped down beside him. "Brrr, it's going to be cold in your teepee tonight. What do you s-say...um," God, she couldn't stand this, couldn't do it. "Say we break out your sleeping bag?"

Clutching his medicine bag in one hand, he touched her cheek with the other. His chin began to tremble and his big dark, beautiful brown eyes grew teary. "Mommy, what's wrong?"

She shook her head, too fast. "Not a thing. I was just...I just got tears thinking how much I love you to bits and pieces."

"I love you, Mommy."

"I CANNOT BELIEVE you are sending my dog to Wyoming."

"I can't believe you're still whining about it."

Garrett polished off his fourth cheeseburger and a soda. He reached over to turn down the blast of the heater in Matt's car.

Parked in the same overgrown driveway Matt had found a block and a half from Kirsten McCourt's house, they'd been listening in on the boys in the band for hours. Their bickering and ruminating made it clear they were nervous about Kirsten's foray into the downtown police station, but they were allowing themselves to get puffed up, flushed with the first signs of success.

Things were heating up. The spooks believed their surveillance was finally beginning to pay off. That any minute, Rawlings and their target, Mc-Court, were going to make the crucial error. Sitting so long there in Guiliani's car, Garrett had willed them to make the call to Loehman himself, but so far, nothing.

Matt was drumming his thumbs on the steering wheel.

"Something wrong, Guili?"

"The prospect of drugging my dog, for one thing."

"If you don't, Wag'll wake up the kid before we get out of the driveway." Garrett yawned. "It's just a sleeping pill. Besides, if you hadn't suggested I take Wag along to the park, Christo wouldn't even know he existed."

"Yeah, well, I'm a sucker for a kid without a dad. What can I say?"

"Not a lot," Garrett wisecracked, because there was a lot of history, a lot of poignant crap bound up in Matt's being a sucker for a kid without a dad.

All of it old news. Just stuff you learned when you spent your life undercover and spent precious few hours connected to your own life.

Times like those, you desperately needed something real to cling to, even if it was painful, even if it was history, especially if it wasn't your own familiar screwed-up terrain.

Everybody had one of those, an inner landscape that, no matter how beautiful, became littered over a lifetime with disappointments, losses, land mines. It was appalling how easy it came to be shared, harder to recall how you came to be the one spilling your guts.

He wadded up the cheeseburger wrap and shoved it into the paper bag. His own past was on the rampage, nagging.

He couldn't remember ever before encountering Kirsten McCourt, but every instinct inside him lobbied against his faulty recall. When he boiled it down, all his impressions, his questions, her answers, his actions, her reactions, and not least, his attraction to her, he realized that everything about the woman clashed with his expectations and his experience, and he didn't like the disparity at all.

She looked fragile but he knew better. Vulnerable, yes, because of Christo. But fragile?

No.

No shrinking violet could have done the things she'd had to do to make the case against Chet Loehman come together five years ago. She had an iron will when push came to shove, yet she'd done a one-hundred-and-eighty-degree turn on the position she'd staked in room five this afternoon.

She was smart. She knew how these things happened. She could have gotten herself and her son into protective custody and been long gone by now. She'd have had to live with the possibility that Loehman would never stop coming after her, but if all this came to a dead end despite its promise, there was a better than even chance that threat would never materialize.

Which meant either that Kirsten McCourt believed they would only half succeed with her there to bait Rawlings, and she'd pay with her life…or that without her they could not succeed at all.

Either way, he admitted to Guiliani, sucking down the last of the melted ice in his cup, she paid.

Wag began to whine and scratch at the back door window to be let out. Glaring at Garrett, because after this pit stop Wag was going to dreamland, Matt switched off the overhead-light toggle and reached behind his seat to open the door and let Wag scramble out unattended. "So what's your problem?"

"She's hiding something."

Matt moved the toothpick in his mouth to one side with his tongue. He didn't answer, which blackened Garrett's mood even more. Guiliani's IQ was in the stratosphere. He thought at about the speed of light, and one-on-one like this, his voluble mouth was never far behind.

"Gee. What do you think it is?" Garrett supplied in a cranky voice, then went silent.

"See," Matt said softly, "if I thought you could answer the question, I'd have asked."

"Thanks for the vote of confidence."

"It's no vote at all, just the truth." Wag wormed

his way back in and Guiliani reached behind to close the door. He took a sleeping pill out of his shirt pocket, broke open the capsule and began mashing the granules into a couple of French fries. "But since you mention it, maybe we need to look at the possibility that she's afraid of you. Maybe she has something to hide."

"Like what?"

Matt tossed Wag the fries, which the poor unsuspecting mutt gobbled without tasting. "Maybe Loehman got to her already. Maybe he's getting tired of us dogging his case, harassing his people. Suppose his real agenda is to sucker us into some trap where we can be…dealt with—"

"Killed off?"

"—in one fell swoop. Yeah." Matt paused to guzzle down high-caffeine-content soda, then went on. "Maybe Burton Rawlings isn't quite the disaffected victim he portrays himself as being. Don't forget, Kirsten McCourt was married to Lane Montgomery, who was already in Loehman's pocket. Maybe Rawlings was, too."

Garrett thought Matt was spinning one doozy of a conspiracy theory. "So then, according to your theory, out of fear for her kid's life, Kirsten is cooperating with Loehman for the purpose of sucking us into some kind of ambush."

"It'd work, Garrett. They set up a phony stakeout across the street designed to make us lick our chops at the potential for striking at the heart of Loehman's operations. We get sucked into their sting operation instead of them getting sucked into ours."

Garrett sent him a look. "You have gone right over the edge, do you know that?"

"One of us has."

"So you're shining me on, here, is that it? Because I think she's hiding something?"

"Not for a minute." Matt clapped his trap shut and stared a few moments out at the surrounding darkness. "I agree. She is afraid of you."

"But you're not seriously saying you believe all that. Not that Loehman wouldn't thrill to the possibility, but this is pretty far out."

"I don't know what to believe, Garrett. Something's not right."

Garrett expelled a frustrated breath. "What's on your mind, *paisan?*"

He expelled one long frustrated breath and reached beneath the seat of his car. He handed Garrett an eight-by-eleven-and-a-half-inch sheet of paper. Garrett angled the sheet toward the street lamps shedding some decent light and saw his own image in near-perfect detail.

"Where did this come from?"

"I found it this afternoon on Kirsten's computer printer, Garrett. It's time-stamped about twelve hours before she took her act to Ann Calder."

Chapter Six

Suddenly, Matt's conspiracy theory took on some credence for Garrett, but his mind was busy spinning excuses for Kirsten McCourt.

Maybe she'd assisted in the destruction of her own evidence years ago. She must have been pregnant with Christo then, vulnerable to Loehman's threats and her own husband's treachery. If she had bowed to the pressure in fear of her own life, if she'd had any part in destroying the evidence, her greatest fear now would be of Garrett's team finally bringing Loehman down. If that happened, all hell would break loose.

Loehman would finger her, giving up her complicity in destroying the evidence in a heartbeat. She'd go to prison and lose her son.

Garrett didn't believe it, but he couldn't afford the luxury of dismissing the print of his own image in her possession, or Kirsten's fear of him. He could think of no other reason for it.

He left Matt sitting in his car, hurdled the chain-link fence and let himself into her back door with Matt's key. He spotted a duffel bag waiting on the landing, filled with what he assumed she'd packed for her son's sojourn. He thought he must know what this was like for her, then admitted to himself he didn't have the foggiest idea. If he had a clue, where would it have come from?

He'd never even heard of a baby monitor.

Once upon a time, he had figured he'd have a couple of babies by now, but then, he'd figured a lot of things that might have been but were never going to be now.

Margo had been his ticket to that life. It alarmed him, that he couldn't even remember what Margo looked like.

Blond, blue-eyed. That much.

He couldn't remember any more, not the shape of her face or the curve of her smile or how he once thought she fit standing next to him. Or even how he'd believed he wouldn't be able to go on living. Not really.

All he could think now as he came upon Kirsten in the study was how he had to stuff his hands into his pockets so he wouldn't give in to the insane urge to cross the room and take Christo's mother into his arms instead of confronting her with the picture of him off her printer.

"Is this," he asked softly, flipping the switch that controlled the small library lamp beside her, "what you're looking for?"

EVEN IN THE inadequate light of the lamp, she could see that Garrett was holding the print of his own reconstructed Identicomp image.

She'd only just remembered it herself, had only come looking for it a few moments ago.

Dread congealed from an amorphous cloud to a solid block of fear in her chest. What was there to say? She'd printed out the image of a man whose name she hadn't even known twenty-four hours ago, but whose name she knew now.

Her heart thudded painfully.

He must know now that Christo was his son. *Wouldn't he know?*

Maybe she'd meant to leave it there on her printer, subconsciously arranged it like that, to let the image speak for itself and for her. Maybe she'd wanted him to come upon his own likeness.

She sank into her chair and looked back at his tightened, hardened profile, unable to believe she had come to this. Scared so bad that she would blame Garrett Weisz for her lies of omission and wish on him a discovery as heartless as that.

She answered his question. "Yes."

"Tell me a story, Kirsten. I'll try real hard to believe."

Her chin went up. All she could think was how terribly handsome he was, how male, how compelling his nose was, how she had chosen to do what she had done. "There is no story."

His head hung for a couple of seconds as if he had to keep a tight rein or shake the truth from her. "An explanation, then. Did Loehman get to you first?"

Loehman? "I don't know what you mean."

His voice low, deliberate, scarcely camouflaging a deep, if unwilling, distrust, he stared at her. "It means I want to know where you got this photo, Kirsten. I need to know where you got it, and when, and I need to know now. Who gave you this picture?''

"No one gave it to me." *What could he be thinking?* She knew suddenly that this was not about Christo, not about the night they had met and made love and conceived together a beautiful little boy.

"No one gave it to you."

Disappointment spread like a stain seeping through her body. "That's right. No one gave it to me. Garrett—"

"Not Rawlings, not Loehman, not the spooks across the street?''

"Garrett, I don't have any idea what you're saying! Do you think I'm somehow in league with *them?* Why? What—''

"Kirsten." He interrupted her, then for a moment, shut his mouth, seeming to consider very carefully what he said to her. "If Christo was threatened by Loehman through Rawlings—or in any other way— there isn't one of us who would blame you for going along with whatever Loehman dictated." She started to interrupt, but he held up a warning hand. "If that's what happened, Kirsten, now is the time to spit it out.''

"Garrett, I swear to you that's not—''

He gave a warning shake of his head. "Too easy, Kirsten.''

"Too easy? My God, do you think this is easy? Can you possibly believe—''

"What I *know* is that there isn't any reasonable explanation for a photo of me to have been printed out on your computer hours ahead of our ever meeting. Not unless you were given the photo and told I was the man you were supposed to get to. Do you have any idea of the odds against your story being true?''

She fell back a bit into her chair, stunned by the perfect logic of it, by the sheer improbability not only of a baby monitor spoiling a stakeout, but of her having in her possession, from her computer, so perfect a photo of Garrett Weisz—unless what he surmised was the truth instead.

For if it was true, then she was even more the sacrificial lamb staked out on the hillside, baiting String's enemies into an ambush that would solve all Loehman's problems, both from within the TruthSayers and without.

Loehman might well have engineered the whole thing.

''I can't speak for Burton Rawlings, but—'' She broke off, trying to assimilate such twisted, protracted revenge. ''It's possible that Loehman was using Burton to get to me. But no one gave me your photo, and what happened with Christo's baby monitor is true. I haven't lied to you, Garrett. Not once.''

But she could see that his doubts were not going away on the strength of her word. She even understood. If Loehman had gotten to her, if he had set up an ambush, if Christo's life had been threatened, she'd have lied to them with the last breath she would ever draw.

''Do you know anything about computers?''

He nodded.

''Then if you want, check out the jpeg files. If

anyone had sent me a photo of you, that's where you'd find it.''

Still leaning against the doorjamb, he crossed his arms over his chest. His face, so handsome, so expressive, so revealed in his own small son, remained impassive.

Shadowed.

Mistrustful.

''Suppose you tell me instead what kind of files I'll find it in.''

''Identicomp—an ICP extension.'' She watched as deepening suspicion flitted across his eyes. The program was used by law enforcement everywhere to generate suspect photos, and it wasn't found on the open market.

Her chin went up. ''It's an old version of the software. I have it because I was involved in ironing out the bugs years ago.''

His broad handsome forehead creased. ''You're telling me you created that photo from stock features?''

''Yes.''

''From descriptions of me?''

She shook her head. ''From memory.''

''What memory, Kirsten?''

The one of the place and time that I knew what it was to be loved. She bit her lip. What she knew was an illusion, a pretense and a poor bargain, to boot, a sacrifice of her *self* for a few hours of something transcendent. For the first time, regret stung her. ''It isn't important.''

''I don't think you want to be deciding for me

what's important, Kirsten. Not now. Not with Christo's well-being at stake.''

For a split second she imagined he did know, that he was toying with her, but then she saw that he meant it in the most literal sense.

''It has nothing to do with anything that's happening now.''

''Kirsten—'' He stopped himself. There was already too much at stake, too many lives, too many threats, too powerful an enemy, and she knew he was aware that she had reason to understand all that with brutal clarity. ''What memory?''

She had no choice but to tell him. Not if he was to believe she wasn't in league with Loehman. But she could barely get the words out, hardly look at him face-to-face. ''I...we met at a...a bar one...one night. A long time ago.''

''How long ago? A year? Two?''

He wasn't going to get it. Wasn't going to look at what was staring him in the face, that it was his own son he was taking from her. ''It was the Mercury. The night—'' She broke off. An unease invaded his posture, darkening his already shadowed eyes. ''The night—''

''I've only been to the Merc once in my life.''

''Then you know what...memory.'' But he gave no indication of remembering her. ''Or not.'' She mocked it herself to prevent him breaking her heart one more time. ''We had a one-night stand.''

He recoiled from the blistering of *one-night stand.* ''Kirsten...I'm not—''

''That kind of man?'' She shrugged, battling back from some abyss even colder yet. ''I'm not that kind of woman, either. But once. You were, once, Garrett. And I was. Once.'' Her throat closed, making that hideous little clicking sound a throat makes when you're trying hard not to cry.

She waited.

And waited. He was staring at his shoes now, his head bowed, his fingers jammed into the pockets of his Levi's. The sea of silence deepened. Could he draw a line between the only two dots that mattered? The wait made what was fluid and vulnerable and honest in her go hard, like seawater drying up, leaving only salt behind in the wounds on her spirit.

He looked up at her again. ''That's all there is to it, then?''

The print, he meant. She meant more. ''Yeah. That's all there is to it.''

He released a pent-up breath. ''It's time, Kirsten.''

A cry flew out of her. She clapped a hand over her mouth, bolted out of her chair and turned away from him.

HE WISHED with all his heart that he knew what to do, how to make this easier, but he had never felt so sucker-punched in his life. The shape of her slender back defined despair. He supposed he'd have had to be a completely heartless bastard not to feel as if he ought to be drawing her into his arms for a moment's respite, but he couldn't.

He was scared spitless.

It all made sense now, or came close. He knew why he'd stood there like a fool, staring at Kirsten McCourt through a two-way with Ross Vorees standing there wondering what was going on. He knew why the scent of her evoked nebulous, half-erotic memories. He knew.

And now he knew they were erotic. Intimate.

From her closed-off posture it was clear to him that she wanted no part of any reassurances he could impart to her, any comfort he could offer. She wanted what he couldn't give her. To have remembered her, remembered *them*. And now she had to hand over to him the most precious piece of her life. *In extremis* was no exaggeration of her state of mind. Nor was it unwarranted.

He didn't even want to examine his own. He didn't have the time. When he did, it wouldn't be a pretty picture.

It didn't matter now. What was important was that Christo had to be gotten out of harm's way.

She sniffed and gulped for a little air. Cries locked in her throat. The biggest favor he could do her was to get it over and done. To take Christo and leave. He sucked in a deep breath, turned and left the study, and took a couple of steps toward her son's room.

She reached out and clutched at his arm. He turned back. He could tell she had to tell him something, that it wasn't an option. He couldn't brush her off, couldn't misread the pleading in her posture.

He stepped back toward her and bent his head low. On tiptoe, she touched his shoulder. Her lips drew near to his ear. "If he wakes up," she breathed, "if he's afraid, tell him I told you our secret password."

On one level he absorbed what she was saying to

him, but her breasts brushed his arm, her breath touched his cheek and he reacted sharply, gripping her arm, staring at her mouth, coping with his swift, fierce arousal. On another level, a dark, heated awareness unlike anything he could remember flared between them.

Of desire long forgotten on his part. It was alive now.

Of dim memory sharpened, but not enough, not nearly enough to grasp.

He saw in her eyes, in the dim glow of a night-light plugged into Christo's bedroom wall, that for her, this moment of giving over her son, this exchange of guardianship of Christo's small, precious life, was an act more intimate than any other.

A small, mewling sound escaped her.

"Kirsten, for the love of God…" His voice, his words, were little more than a harsh breath.

She looked away, anywhere but at him.

He didn't understand.

He knew sexual desire. He knew its tricks, its effect, its fulfillment, pleasure, pain, resolution. He knew its every nuance. Not in recent times but over the course of a marriage he could only vaguely re-call now. But this tension, the power of this thing between Kirsten and him, he didn't understand. The thought glanced through the corridors of his mind that he hadn't understood it that night, either.

He let go a silent breath. No matter that an aeon or more had passed between them, no more than a minute could have gone by in real time. "What is it?" he breathed. "The secret password."

She swallowed. "Snow Dancer." Shivering, she

took another step back. "She's one of the carousel horses at the park in Spokane." A small gulp. "Christo's favorite."

Garrett nodded and turned away, forcing aside emotions he couldn't define or even recognize. Sinking to one knee, he bent low and saw as he flashed a small penlight inside the dark confines of a teepee that her small son lay curled inside a sleeping bag.

He pocketed the penlight, came up and sank again to his haunches. Pulling the uppermost edge of the downy thickness, he slid the sleeping bag and sleeping child onto his lap. Cradling the little boy in his arms, Garrett pivoted in his crouch and stood.

She stepped forward, toward Garrett, and looked at her tiny son sleeping peacefully, undisturbed. Cupping the crown of his head, she bent over him, bringing her cheek to Christo's.

He found himself holding Christo's dead weight, at least thirty-five pounds, in one arm, and brought the other hand up to touch her, to close a circle that somehow needed closing. But the silky feel of her hair, the way she smelled, the depth of emotion and power of her will beneath it, the child between them—all of it closed a gap inside himself as well. A gap where tenderness might once have been found to reside.

As if she feared what he might read into allowing his touch, she backed off. The gap split open inside him again.

Their eyes met briefly. He transferred the bulk of Christo's weight to his other arm. Behind him, from somewhere inside the teepee, she brought out a leather drawstring pouch and tucked it deep down inside Christo's sleeping bag.

Dry-eyed, she turned on her heel and started down the stairs with the duffel bag. At the back door, she unzipped the bag and put in a pair of overshoes, then handed the bag over to Garrett and opened the door.

So far as he knew, she watched their progress until she couldn't see them anymore.

AT MIDNIGHT, Guiliani, Thorne, Vorees and a couple of men she hadn't met stormed her house, staging the kidnapping.

Kirsten worried that her performance was flat, that she wasn't delivering anything like the agony and hysteria she should be experiencing if at that moment Christo was stripped from her arms.

If she'd felt out of control all those hours ago, she had no words to describe what she felt now, with Christo gone, carried off into the night.

Emotionless, maybe. Colorless. Hopeless. She wasn't an actor, and she couldn't summon the fury she should be feeling. Her fury was submerged. She couldn't reach it, couldn't tap into it, couldn't dredge up one fiery emotion. Her baby was long since gone, taken with her complete cooperation.

Encouraging her, egging her on, J.D. jerked a chair from the dining set across the hardwood floor, making a terrible, careless racket. "Sit down—"

"You will never get away with this," she whispered, coming a little alive. "Who are you?"

"Sit down," he snarled, his expression softening the impact for her. "And shut up. I'm doing the talking here. Is that clear to you?"

"Perfectly."

From behind Vorees now, J.D. nodded again. Matt Guiliani, the one who had seemed so completely sympathetic to her at the police station, wasn't even looking at her. He and Vorees both wore headphones, listening to the effect their assault on her house and theft of her child were having on the watchers across the street. Grim satisfaction on his face, Vorees lifted his thumb like a rocket going straight up, and mouthed, "Ballistic."

"Good." J.D. barked in answer to that, though seeming to acknowledge her understanding that he was the one in charge. "You understand, I understand, we all understand. Isn't that swell? So this, sweet darlin', is what's going down from here on out."

J.D. went through the charade just as Garrett had explained it hours ago, this time for the benefit of Loehman's watchers across the street. "So you see. You get the kid back when we get what we want. Fair enough?"

She shut her eyes. It took no special effort to cause the waver in her voice. "I don't know what you want from me—"

J.D.'s fist came down so hard on her dining-room table that her grandmother's antique silver candlesticks skittered. "Is that really the line you want to take with me, lady?" He shrugged, sitting there at the table like an actor on first read-through of a script, miming gestures, no intensity in his features, only the voice.

"I don't know, guys, what do you think? Maybe she don't want her kid back?" Vorees added.

"Don't be such an ass," Guiliani snapped, playing out the scenario, but to Kirsten he looked really very dangerous. "Look, you've got her scared out of her gourd already. We didn't drive three hundred miles thinking to be back tomorrow," he said, dropping the hint that they'd come from the Tri-Cities area. "Lay off a while, huh? The dame knows what's what here."

"What's your problem?" J.D. demanded, looking truly puzzled at Matt.

For a couple of minutes the two of them clashed heatedly, role-playing, calling each other by names she assumed were known members of the Tri-Cities splinter group. They created a powerful illusion of men who, if they were tired and on edge, were nevertheless single-mindedly focused on their plan to hold her child hostage until they got what they wanted.

But watching them she sensed a subtext she didn't understand, an impression that where J.D. was satisfied with the way things were going, Matt Guiliani was not.

He finally broke it off. Both of the additional men brought in to support the ruse added their two cents' periodically, had a beer and announced now that they were going off for some shut-eye. Kirsten knew from the soft sounds of the door closing off the back porch that they'd gone.

Vorees made himself at home on the sofa, guzzling bottled water, flipping through the newspaper, which left her with J.D. and Matt Guiliani at the dining-room table. J.D. pulled a legal pad out of a backpack and they traded notes for a while.

What time, she wrote, *will my friends have Christo?*

2:00 to 3:00 a.m. They'll call you. You're doing fine.

She shrugged. *Should we be talking? Won't silence make them suspicious?*

Try not to worry about them or what they think. Best thing is to be yourself in crisis.

I'd be trying to get them to talk to me.

Go for it.

"Where did you come from?" she asked aloud.

"What's that supposed to mean?" He wrote, *Kansas. You?*

She smiled. "The other guy said you drove three hundred miles." She paused, scribbling *Boston* was her hometown. "That's a long way to come to kidnap a child." *College?*

"Well, not just any child would do, now, would it?" he asked nastily.

She let a beat or two pass, as if shocked to silence by the cruelty, while J.D. scribbled. *Same. KU. Typical studly athlete. Jayhawks wide receiver.*

She smiled, then asked a question for which, more than anything, she wanted the answer. "I don't even know what you want from me. How will you know," she asked softly, scribbling *How will they know,* "when you've got what you want so I can have my son back?"

She had no idea how he could both follow what he was hearing through the earphones and her exchange with J.D., but Matt answered her question. "If it comes from Rawlings, it's what we want."

Nodding, J.D. agreed.

"How do you *know* that? How could you possibly know that Burton Rawlings has anything you want?"

J.D. sighed heavily. "Lady, will you just shut your yap? Trust me on this. When we've got what we want, we'll know it." Meanwhile, J.D. sketched himself with a Schwarzenegger body, lantern jaw, pea brain.

She nearly laughed aloud. *You're good.*

Artist? Nah.

Her throat tightened. The air seemed too thick to breathe, too choked with hidden meaning, lies, out-right deception, clever half-truths, but for just that second, J.D.'s caricature had eased her heart.

Company, I meant. Tears blurred her vision. *Good company.*

J.D. tilted his head back and forth, no big deal. *Thanks.*

She felt suddenly spent, finally at the end of her rope. "I'm going to bed. If that's all right with you."

"You do that. But take my advice. Don't lie awake trying to figure out a way to double-cross us."

"With my son's life at stake?"

J.D. shrugged. "I'm just saying."

Looking steadily at her, Matt took the headset off. "Sweet dreams." No wink, no encouraging nod. Just…sweet dreams.

J.D. scribbled that they would let her know when the call came in from her friends, and she nodded. But Matt's refusal to temper his words with the smallest gesture of kindness filled her with unease.

Telling herself to ignore it, she went upstairs and climbed into bed still wearing jeans and a sweater.

The clock on the nightstand, where Christo's baby monitor was missing, read 1:40 and she didn't know where her little boy was.

Chapter Seven

Flying eastbound, their course taking them over some of the world's most spectacular mountain ranges in the dark of night, Garrett had little to do save examine his state of mind. Christo had not awakened even in the transfer from Guiliani's car to the jet, or during the takeoff. With Wag tight up against the sleeping bag and zonked himself, Christo still slept peacefully.

Snow Dancer.

For some reason, images of the carousel horses in Spokane resided in Garrett's own memory. He had never been there, never had a sunny, carefree afternoon with any child in a park of any description. The twenty minutes he'd spent with Kirsten in the park while Wag and Christo played was the sum total of his experience. But at some time or other he must have seen photographs of the carousel horses in a newspaper or on a billboard.

The detail was a wildly extraneous one. What was the use of knowing how he knew about carousel horses?

But he couldn't help chewing on the likelihood

that at some point in time he had also mistakenly dismissed as irrelevant critical information concerning Christo McCourt's mother.

He'd been over it a hundred times, over her employment dossier till he knew it by heart.

He knew the day Lane Montgomery died.

He knew her birth date and Christo's, her professional history and contacts, her personal friends, her job, Christo's immunization record and the one trip to the E.R. to stitch up a cut under his chin.

Acquainted with more details, in possession of more real substance than he believed necessary to add two and two together and come up with four, Garrett was at a loss.

At some point, crossing the Rockies, watching Kirsten's irrepressible, handsome little boy sleeping in light reflected from the moon and again off the clouds, Garrett came back around to the explanation that fit the facts.

He and Kirsten McCourt had met before. Not only met, but made love.

Standing in the dark with her holding her son between them, it had to have been the reverberations of that meeting, whenever it had been, whatever the reason, however it had happened, pounding through him. He'd known before she ever uttered the name of the Mercury that it had been no random meeting between them in the course of investigations shared by the U.S. Attorney's office and the naval intelligence liaison task force, no casual encounter reaching for the same newspaper, that Kirsten was not some girl he'd stood up somewhere along the line. In fact, he knew there was sex involved.

In all the time since that night, working with J.D. and Matt, Garrett was the one steadfastly, inhumanly aloof to the wiles of females. Come-on-proof.

Inside twelve hours, no, inside a *single* hour, exhibiting no feminine wiles and the polar opposite of a come-on, Kirsten McCourt had ended all that. He was attracted to her, *by* her, on every level, and J.D. had seen it.

There was sex, all right, but there was more. Far more, and Garrett only glimpsed how bad it was when he found himself thinking that when this was all over, he would take Christo and his mother east to Spokane to visit Snow Dancer. Maybe north, too, because he knew there was another restored carousel somewhere outside Victoria.

In all his life, he'd never imagined such an outing. Not even in the time of Margo. Even then he'd understood he loved her too much, too hard, too hot. Plagued from the first with the notion that Margo, well-bred, high-born trust-fund baby that she was, had been slumming with him, he'd convinced himself the marriage would last anyway. There was slumming, and then there was slumming.

He was an officer and a gentleman, highly decorated.

But he suspected now that with Margo, trips to the park to feed the ducks or visit the carousel horses would have been parceled out to the resident nanny.

The copilot stuck his head into the cabin and advised they'd be landing within ten minutes. He kept his voice low for the sake of the sleeping child. "Weather advisories are poor. There's a blizzard coming down out of Canada. You'll only have an hour, maybe ninety minutes if we're lucky, before we have to get out.''

Garrett nodded. ''I assume there's ground transportation waiting?'' It would take every available moment to drive Christo to the Wilders' and make the return trip.

''Yes. The state highway patrol, an unmarked four-wheel drive.''

Christo stirred twice in the next hour, once meeting the icy cold blast of wind as Garrett carried him off the jet, then again, as Garrett trekked through six inches of snow already fallen in the starkly moonlit mountain meadow where Sam and Ginny Wilder now lived.

He carried Kirsten's sleeping son through the darkened house up to the spare bedroom. Ginny Wilder had turned the covers aside, but Garrett laid Christo down on the bed still in his sleeping bag. Christo stretched and sighed, scrubbing in his sleep at his nose with a small fist, then stuck the tiny thumb in his mouth.

In the silence, watching Christo by the dim light from the hallway, Garrett heard the sweet small sucking noises. He sank down, mesmerized by the sound of it and the image that came out of no experience he knew of the infant Christo suckling at Kirsten's breast.

Against a fierce arousal, another regret for which he had no name laid itself up in his heart.

He rose and pushed past Ginny Wilder and took the stairs down two at a time. Her husband was letting Wag inside. Garrett pulled a digital phone from the pocket of his parka and gave it to Sam, briefly explaining from some distant, separate self what was going on, and that they should use the digital cell to call Kirsten.

In their good-hearted, lined and weary faces he found deep anxiety for Kirsten's life. "I won't insult your intelligence with half-baked reassurances," he told them. "Kirsten is in real danger, but we're doing everything we can. You have my word on that."

On the treacherous drive back down the mountain, he had a conversation with the state highway patrolman at the wheel.

A talk that made his blood run as cold as the air fronting the Arctic storm.

Despite the protection of the feds, the wife of the sheriff who'd busted up the illegal assembly of TruthSayers, not a hundred miles from the Wilders', lay close to death in the hospital. Her back was broken when her car was forced off the road and into a ravine of a thousand feet and only a few sparse lodgepole pine.

The federal agent assigned to the sheriff's wife was dead on impact.

Loehman, Garrett thought, choosing his venue, thumbing his nose, upping the stakes.

Destroying people's lives.

But the inescapable truth of his own besotted, dishonorable behavior on that cold winter's night nearly five years ago blotted even Loehman's crimes from Garrett's mind.

JUST OVER THREE HUNDRED miles to the north, Chet Loehman would never conceive of what he was about in such terms. He understood that the ignorant and the misguided, along with an ever-shrinking number of men and women in law enforcement, believed such rubbish, but he was about the people's business, pure and simple, whether they were capable of appreciating the fact or not.

He puttered around a bit in his kitchen, pouring a brandy, choosing a shortbread cookie for accompaniment, the food he ate and the drink he drank as unembellished as his philosophy.

Freedom should be that simple. Abuse it, lose it.

Justice should be just that unfettered. Swift, deliberate, uncomplicated. That was what the country needed.

How many more times did the system have to fail so spectacularly to convict blatant, unrepentant, swaggering murderers before the masses awoke?

He bit into the cookie, but along with the anger slowly ebbing out of his system, his guard let down as well. The toothache he'd been nursing for weeks at the hands of an inept dentist sent waves of pain shooting through the right half of his jaw, and all his resentments came rushing right back.

As it had turned out, he should have ordered the sudden and unexpected demise of Burton Rawlings when the worm first stumbled over his find. It infuriated Loehman that the swift and certain justice he championed would have stamped Paid to the Montgomery debacle. The man was a conniving liar, playing both ends against the middle such that even now his treachery threatened everything Loehman had worked for over thirty years to build.

How could he have known? He couldn't.

But now he would have to let the play unfold to

its lumbering and far less certain end. There was nothing else to do. He had to deal not only with this threat, but with the would-be kings who thought they could run his organization better. Then he must return to the business of bringing the country back to its senses. Law enforcement wasn't even stemming the tide of crime, never mind turning it back.

Vigilante justice, the justice of the common man, was the only real justice to be had at the dawn of the new millennium.

He hurled the remainder of the shortbread cookie into the wastebasket, then swallowed the contents of his snifter. As the brandy burned its way down his gullet, it lit other old resentments.

Kirsten McCourt, God love her.

He'd cut her every imaginable slack though she was the one most responsible for the evidence against him five years ago. Still, she was only a female, and he'd allowed her to live and now she was right back in the thick of Rawlings's plot to destroy him.

He wasn't deeply worried, only powerfully offended by her staggering ingratitude. He had friends in high places, but he could only go to certain wells so many times before they ran dry.

Kirsten McCourt must learn, once and for all time, exactly what it meant to her to cross him.

WHEN GARRETT GOT BACK from Wyoming, Kirsten was sleeping. He'd caught a little shut-eye on the return trip, damned little. Not enough. He needed a coffee, a shower, a shave and a reprieve in that order, but when he came through the front door as if he owned the place, he changed his mind, snagged Matt's attention with a jerk of his head and went back out onto the porch.

"How'd it go?" Matt asked.

"Without a hitch." Garrett sat down on the top step.

"That's good." Matt sat down beside him. "Isn't that good?"

"Yeah. That's good."

"So…what's not so good?"

Garrett squinted off into the distance.

He wanted Loehman badly enough that in the last hour or so, Garrett had come to the conclusion that he had to step aside. His objectivity was shot to kingdom come, and if by some slipup, some miscue, some poor call he made because he was thinking of Kirsten McCourt or her small son ahead of the job, he wouldn't be able to live with himself.

So he looked his best friend in the eye and told him, "I have to take myself off the case."

Matt stared at him slack-jawed. "What's this about, Garrett?"

He gave a scoff. "Fitness for duty."

"You're right. You've lost it." Matt frowned. "Tell me this isn't about Kirsten." He'd heard the gist of the story driving Garrett and Christo and Wag the dog to the airport.

"I'm serious, *paisan.*"

"So am I," Matt snapped. "Think again. Go ahead. Take your time. Just think again and then forget it."

"I am thinking. I know it's not quite up to your speed—"

Matt swore succinctly. "Whatever you call what you're doing, it's not thinking. Wallowing, maybe. What is it with you? We are closer to nailing Loehman than we've ever been—"

"We aren't even in the neighborhood, Matt—"

"—and you're telling me you're ready to take yourself out of the game over lust for Kirsten McCourt?"

He'd clenched his teeth for so many hours, his jaw ached. He focused through the trees and over the slanting roofs of houses till he could glimpse sunlight reflecting off the surface of Lake Union. "That's what I'm telling you."

"I've never heard anything half so chickenhearted in my entire misbegotten life."

"I'm not telling you I'm pulling the plug. I'm telling you I'm not the one who should be running the show."

"Please. Spare me the subtle distinctions. The two are one and the same, and you know it. We'll lose any edge we have if we have to gear down long enough to bring someone else up to speed, so if you want my advice you'll suck it up and do what you have to do."

"This *is* what I have to do."

"No. This is a cop-out. So what if Kirsten McCourt had herself a roll in the hay one night five years ago and you were there. So what? You want to try explaining to me how some one-night stand you don't even remember compromises your ability to run this operation?"

"If a one-night stand wasn't poor judgment enough to convince you by itself, bud, I don't know what will." But he felt a nasty twist occurring in his gut. Even as he mocked his own poor judgment, he knew that what he'd taken away from that night was insight that had turned his life inside out.

He'd loved his wife, head over heels, but he'd never gotten from her in all the years of their marriage what he got from Kirsten in a few hours in the dark of night.

Matt swore softly. "Garrett, it was five years ago. But just for argument's sake, call it five *days* ago. Say you're besotted. Say you've really gone round the bend for her. What would it change? How would this go down any different? Just say it all comes down to saving Kirsten's life or bringing Loehman in. There isn't even a debate. Loehman walks. Every one of us would make that choice. That's what separates us from him, right? What makes us the guys in the white hats? We do the right thing, even when it costs us the whole enchilada.

"Besides," he cracked, grinning, shoving Garrett with his elbow, "objectivity is highly overrated."

Garrett said nothing, only sat staring at his hands, still offended at his own behavior. Where was the honor in him, to have let himself take a woman to bed whose name he didn't even know?

"So am I preaching to the choir, here, or just to myself?"

Garrett shook his head. "I can't risk it, Guili. I won't."

Matt's complexion darkened in a way only anger caused. "Okay. Put this into your pity pipe and smoke it, then. If you pull out, Weisz, I quit."

Garrett stiffened, his tone unbending, his eyes firing back. "Don't threaten me, Guili."

Matt shook his head. "That was no threat, *paisan.* That is a fact." He stood and glared down at Garrett. "For the record, there's something else you should know." He shut his mouth and jammed his fingers into the front pockets of his jeans and it took him another several seconds to get to the place where he could say what he had to say.

"I would rather rip out my heart with my bare hands than walk out on you."

WHEN SHE WOKE, Kirsten showered briefly, dressed in jeans and the simple but extravagantly expensive barely pink mohair sweater she considered comfort clothing and went down to the kitchen, heading for a cup of freshly brewed coffee. From the bottom of the stairs she could see Garrett and Matt through the screen door, sitting together, their dark heads close, deep in conversation.

She had no idea whether Garrett would tell Matt why she had the photo in the first place. He must. Matt had to have been the one who'd found Garrett's photo print in her study.

J.D. was sitting at the dining-room table reading the newspaper, looking surprisingly fresh for a night spent without sleep. He looked up as she paused by the foot of the stairs.

She angled her head toward the porch. "What's going on?"

He pointed to his ear and across the street to remind her to watch what she said. He shook his head, indicating that he didn't know what was happening with Garrett and Matt, then struck a nasty tone for the benefit of the boys in the band. "Doesn't concern you."

"Everything concerns me," she returned. "Isn't that the point?"

"No. What concerns you is keeping your trap shut till you have something useful to say." He made a face at her. "Think you can remember that?"

Her eyes wouldn't stop flitting back to the backs of the men on the porch. "I'll keep it in mind."

"There's a good idea."

Passing the table, she went into the kitchen and poured herself a cup of coffee. Through the side window, she saw Guiliani get up, stand over Garrett for a couple of seconds, then turn and bang through the screen door. He headed straight for the kitchen, nearly colliding with her, taken aback to find her standing there.

Shorter than Garrett by a couple of inches, Matt still loomed over her. "You want to get out of the way, or hand me a mug."

She turned on her heel, put her own coffee down, then brought out two mugs from the cabinet. He took one from her and poured his own coffee, set down the pot as Garrett walked in behind him. He looked straight at her as she handed the remaining mug to Garrett.

He poured coffee as well, then turned around in the unnaturally silent kitchen and leaned against the counter, sucking down the coffee. Matt turned and walked out, leaving her alone with Garrett.

She didn't know what to say or how to escape or

whether she should, not only because of the bugs. Garrett wouldn't look at her, only stood staring at the floor. She knew he must have told Guiliani about the Mercury.

Her heart pounded. Despite the years that had elapsed and all her fears, all her doubts, she knew her attraction to Garrett Weisz that night in the Mercury had been not only a physical one that remained even now, even in this moment, but one that drew her for the right reasons as well.

Garrett Weisz was a man bound by a certain honor, a man who had stepped in with no thought of some sordid sexual payoff, but of protecting her from the drunken lout in the Mercury.

He'd loved his wife.

He'd worked all these years toward extinguishing the power of men like Chet Loehman.

And he'd warned her in the park against mistaking him for a soft touch. He wasn't soft. He couldn't afford to be soft, not when it came to doing what had to be done, but he was easy. He was a man who would do the honorable thing every time—and that was what she thought she saw coming.

And the last thing she wanted.

Her throat tightened. Tears wavered in her eyes. Not unaware of her distress, he reached back to put down his coffee mug. His hand, surely unwitting, went to his chest, over his heart, and he looked at her with a kindness that should have eased her distress, but magnified it instead. "I want you to go upstairs and write down the name of every person you know who ever associated with Burton Rawlings."

"All right." She moved to refill her mug. He moved to accommodate her. She took the mug and fled up the stairs to her study.

He followed her out of the kitchen, but no farther, letting her go because Matt was sitting on the sofa, his feet up on the coffee table, his arms crossed over his chest, waiting. Watching.

He leaned against the door frame. He didn't know what to do. He knew that with the wrong move in this moment, Matt would walk out the door in the next.

The prospect shook him to his core.

He needed to talk to Kirsten, needed somehow to put to rights a situation that had been turned on its head from the start, and somehow, that superseded even making peace with Matt. But then he realized that's why Matt was still sitting there anyway. His friend would cut him that hour of slack, before he delivered on his promise to quit.

J.D. fell back in his chair and pulled the earphones off his head, tossing them onto Kirsten's scarred dining-room table. "Mind letting me in on what's going down here?" he asked, unconcerned that the question would raise any suspicion across the street, visibly suspicious of the evidence he saw of an impending break in their ranks.

"Strategy," Garrett barked.

"You thinking of pulling outta here?"

"No."

J.D. exhaled sharply, although knowing no more than he knew before, looking somewhat reassured. "Let me guess. You'll let me know if anything changes."

Nodding, Garrett pulled off his sweatshirt and tossed it over the back of the chair opposite J.D. where his parka already lay. "You'll be the first."

He grabbed fresh clothes and his straight-edge razor from his duffel bag and went upstairs to shower. At some deeply personal level, he felt he could not go to Kirsten unclean in any sense.

He closed himself off in the bathroom they all used, where Christo's bath toys lined the tub, only to realize there was no shower. He felt foiled, deeply thwarted in his desire to come clean, to *be* clean with Kirsten. She deserved that much from him. What he felt for her—whether reverberations of a night he only vaguely recalled or of the night before, or even of the moment he stood watching Christo peacefully sucking his thumb in his sleep—demanded that much.

But all he could do was strip his T-shirt off over his head, run the hot tap and duck his head under the water. He soaped himself, his face and chest and armpits, scraped the razor over his beard, wiped his torso dry and donned the clean shirt, then combed his hair. But looking himself in the eye in a shabby little mirror made charming by a painted-on frame and the words *I am a star,* he knew the stain on his honor remained.

Kirsten sat in the chair at her computer, bent over the list of names she'd obviously begun to write out by hand, with pen and paper. He moved into the study and picked up the ladder-back chair from the corner in one hand. Setting it down beside her, a few feet away, he sat with her, face-to-face, much

GET A FREE TEDDY BEAR...

You'll love this plush, cuddly Teddy Bear, an adorable accessory for your dressing table, bookcase or desk. Measuring 5 ½" tall, he's soft and brown and has a bright red ribbon around his neck – he's completely captivating! And he's yours *absolutely free*, when you accept this no-risk offer!

AND TWO FREE BOOKS!

Here's a chance to get **two free Harlequin Intrigue® novels** from the Harlequin Reader Service® absolutely free!

There's no catch. You're under no obligation to buy anything. We charge nothing – ZERO – for your first shipment. And you don't have to make any minimum number of purchases – not even one!

Find out for yourself why thousands of readers enjoy receiving books by mail from the Harlequin Reader Service®. They like the **convenience of home delivery**...they like getting the best new novels months before they're available in bookstores...and they love our **discount prices!**

Try us and see! Return this card promptly. We'll send your free books and a free Teddy Bear, under the terms explained on the back. We hope you'll want to remain with the reader service – but the choice is always yours!

381 HDL CTKC   **181 HDL CTJY**
                                                          (H-I-11/99)

Name: _____

(PLEASE PRINT)

Address: _____ Apt.#: _____

City: _____ State/Prov.: _____ Postal Zip/Code: _____

Offer limited to one per household and not valid to current Harlequin Intrigue® subscribers. All orders subject to approval. © 1998 HARLEQUIN ENTERPRISES LTD.
® and ™ are trademarks owned by Harlequin Enterprises Ltd.   **PRINTED IN U.S.A.**

NO OBLIGATION TO BUY!

The Harlequin Reader Service® — Here's how it works:

Accepting your 2 free books and gift places you under no obligation to buy anything. You may keep the books and gift and return the shipping statement marked "cancel." If you do not cancel, about a month later we'll send you 4 additional novels and bill you just $3.34 each in the U.S., or $3.71 each in Canada, plus 25¢ delivery per book and applicable taxes if any.* That's the complete price and — compared to the cover price of $3.99 in the U.S. and $4.50 in Canada — it's quite a bargain! You may cancel at any time, but if you choose to continue, every month we'll send you 4 more books, which you may either purchase at the discount price or return to us and cancel your subscription.

*Terms and prices subject to change without notice. Sales tax applicable in N.Y. Canadian residents will be charged applicable provincial taxes and GST.

If offer card is missing write to: Harlequin Reader Service, 3010 Walden Ave., P.O. Box 1867, Buffalo, NY 14240-1867

BUSINESS REPLY MAIL
FIRST-CLASS MAIL   PERMIT NO. 717   BUFFALO, NY

POSTAGE WILL BE PAID BY ADDRESSEE

HARLEQUIN READER SERVICE
3010 WALDEN AVE
PO BOX 1867
BUFFALO NY 14240-9952

NO POSTAGE
NECESSARY
IF MAILED
IN THE
UNITED STATES

as he had in Vorees's interrogation room less than twenty-four hours before.

"Kirsten." She set aside the pen and paper. Her usual grace of movement seemed to have vanished. She looked at him with such foreboding, such brittle grit that he lost whatever it was he had been about to say.

She fed him the line and then forbade him to use it. "If you say you're sorry for what happened between us that night, I won't ever forgive you." She left him staring, uncomprehending. "And if you say to me that you want to do the honorable thing—"

"Kirsten, cut it out." He shoved a hand through his still-damp hair. Nothing could have prepared him for her forbidding the slightest apology. "What am I supposed to do? Tell you I'm not sorry that I didn't remember you? You think I shouldn't be sorry that I didn't even know your name? Am I supposed to believe you feel nothing at all about that?"

Her head shook slowly back and forth in denial, then dipped low so he couldn't see her eyes anymore. "I would never say what happened between us that night meant nothing to me."

"Then what—"

"It meant everything."

Chapter Eight

"Everything." His breath locked in his chest. The fleeting thought rose in him that she intended not only that the knife be plunged into his heart, but buried as well, twisted without mercy. His jaw clenched. "So the night meant nothing to me, everything to you."

She shrugged artlessly. "Everything I wanted. I never—"

"What did you want?"

Her chin went up. "I wanted what Margo had."

"My wife?" A chill arose in him he couldn't begin to halt, for if she thought she had gotten from him anything Margo had ever known, she was dead wrong.

"Your wife. Yes. I wanted what your wife had. I wanted to *be* her. I wanted to know what it was like to make love with a man who was desperately in love with me. I thought I would never find it for myself, and I...I haven't."

"Kirsten, come on—"

"No—let me finish. That night at the Mercury, I *chose* to let myself believe that if I could be her for you, for one last night together, then I could have what I wanted with all my heart as well.

"I swear to you, I never, ever expected to see you again, or dreamed that if I did, you would remember me. If anyone should apologize, it should be me. But I'm not going to say I'm sorry, because if it had never happened, I wouldn't have—"

A rough knock sounded on the open door. Garrett snapped, "Beat it," without even looking in that direction, but outside the white-noise barrier his warning went unheard and unheeded.

Matt stepped inside the study. "You're wanted downtown."

"Wanted where?"

"Grenallo just called. He wants to be brought up to speed. Now."

Unused to being dragged off—even by a U.S. attorney—to explain himself in the midst of any operation ever, Garrett got up. "How in the Sam Hill does he know there is anything to be brought up to speed about?"

Matt blinked. "One of two possibilities. Rawlings gave up all other avenues and went straight to the top, or else the pilot you conscripted might have mentioned an overnight trip to Wyoming."

Hands on his hips, Garrett jerked his head, signaling an exit to Matt. "Get out, would you please?"

His friend left.

Garrett turned away from Kirsten as well, and went to the window. Holding himself stiff-armed out from the window frame, watching for a seaplane he could hear in the distance, he fought to understand what fatally flawed perception he had of the night, and that Kirsten had harbored all these years about Margo.

He had to go. He dropped his arm and turned back to her. He didn't have time to explain much of anything, even if he could, even if he understood it himself, but he had one thing he had to say now.

"It's true I loved my wife. It's true I don't remember your face, but it's not true that I don't remember you. And if you thought, Kirsten, that I was making love to Margo that night, you were wrong."

ONE OF THEM was always with her, sometimes two, while the others came and went. If three of them were gone, one had taken her car, and the other two took off in vehicles they'd supposedly driven to Seattle from the Tri-Cities. All of their efforts concentrated on finding Burton Rawlings, a man who should not have been possessed of any special skills in pulling off a disappearing act.

She didn't see Garrett again for the next two days, and when the morning of the third day came, Matt told her Garrett wouldn't be back until early evening.

He'd rigged another white-noise barrier to the bugs that while still transmitting the kitchen background noise, the clatter of dishes and silver, the rush of running water, filtered out the range of voices. But as she stood at the griddle turning out piles of pancakes, Matt hovering nearby, the silence between them lengthened. "You feeding an army?"

"It gives me something to do." She missed Christo every minute of the day. She hadn't been able to get through on the cell phone to Ginny and Sam to talk to her son since the first morning. And Lord knew, anything that took her mind for a few moments from ruminating over Garrett's last words to her was a blessing.

Leaning against the refrigerator, Matt shifted, crossing one boot over the other. "Why didn't you tell him about Christo?"

Preparing a couple of plates, doling out crisp bacon and pancakes, her hands went unnaturally still. Her throat made that clicking sound again. She forced herself to resume, to pour warmed syrup into a pitcher, but no clever answer offered itself up. She put down the Depression-glass pitcher before it slipped from her hands. Still turned away, she braced herself with both hands against the counter. "I don't know. I will. I—"

He made some nearly sympathetic sound. "Save it, Kirsten. Till this is over. He doesn't need the distraction now."

He took the plates she'd prepared and left the kitchen.

She stayed, stricken by the deep irony that his best friend had gleaned what Garrett had not. She'd thought he was coming back to her to do the honorable thing, to marry his son's mother because it was the right thing to do. But it wasn't until hours after he'd departed to deal with John Grenallo that she realized he was only making the case that what had happened between them meant more to him than a one-night stand. She'd nearly gotten so far as to overcome the disappointment clogging her throat, to do the honorable thing herself and tell him.

Now another forty-eight hours had passed since she'd seen him. Now she had it in her head that Garrett had not been oblivious to her in that hotel room. Now some gentle breeze of thought wended its way through her mind and body, stirring hope and other dangerous feelings.

The hours dragged by between her calls to Christo, who was as close to seventh heaven as he could be while she wasn't around. He was enthralled with the snow, the tractor to move the snow out of the driveway, Wag the dog's constant antics, his Aunt Ginny's to spoil. She'd fashioned a "manly" unbreakable satin cord and colored it bronze and Christo was wearing his daddy's medallion now.

Garrett kept Grenallo informed, not only supplying him with the cell-phone numbers they were each using, but play-by-play as well. Grenallo wanted results this time, because if he didn't get them, he was going to have to shut down the pursuit of Chet Loehman altogether.

She listened in on J.D.'s earphones a while, enough to learn that the boys in the band were spread too thin to follow three different vehicles, which angered them no end.

They figured they'd been trumped or even dealt out of a game they could not stop hanging around to watch. The ante was very high, and at the last, they figured to ambush the winner and be off with the goods—whatever they were, however they could be leveraged in the battle for control of the TruthSayers organization.

But Rawlings hadn't attempted to contact her again, just as she'd warned them. She spent the first few hours after Garrett left to go talk to John Grenallo with Matt working up Identicomp photos of the three men Matt had seen in the stakeout house. Ross Vorees dropped in, using the back door, to take away a diskette containing the photo files.

He'd planned to try importing the photos into the city, state and national databases, searching for names, matches to rap sheets, connections to Loehman that could also be exploited. But he took one look at the photo prints themselves, handed them back to her and sat on Christo's step stool.

"I know these guys. Two of them anyway."

J.D., this time, was in the study with Kirsten and Vorees. "Who are they?"

"Cops. Tacoma cops."

J.D. shook his head. "Why doesn't that surprise me?"

Feeling slightly ill, Kirsten frowned. "What do you mean?"

"Simple," Vorees answered. "To be honest, it's really not all that cut-and-dried, Kirsten, but we're beginning to see cops overrepresented in vigilante organizations. When you have to watch your righteous collars put back on the streets day in and day out, the years of it begin to tell.

"You harden up," he went on, "till you find you're Andy Sipowicz, only this is real life. You know if the perps go up for something they didn't do, nine times out of ten they should've been in the slammer *before* the crime they didn't commit. To be honest, it's just a matter of time before doling out your own justice begins to look like the only solution."

He gave a small snort, shaking his head. "Imagine these guys getting busted by a baby monitor. Which, by the by, I'm no expert, but what *was* Christo still doing with one of those things? He's four years old, isn't he?"

She felt immediately on the defensive. Ginny had asked her the same thing, with the same result, but Vorees somehow made her feel worse. "Do you have any idea how insensitive that sounds, Detective? Particularly since there *are* bogeymen across the street."

"Those guys wouldn't hurt a kid—"

"But that's not the point, is it?"

"No," Vorees admitted. "You're right. I didn't mean to be such a clod. To be honest, Calder tells me I'm beyond redemption." He made a rueful face. "I think she means it, too."

Kirsten smiled briefly. If he qualified himself one more time with "to be honest," she was going to scream. "I'm…I'm probably much too touchy."

"Not at all, as it turns out. You're right."

He took off then and she spent several hours on the phone calling around to every mutual acquaintance of Burton Rawlings she could think of.

She had no luck.

If Rawlings had intended to hand off evidence to her for safekeeping or any other of a half-dozen possible reasons, he'd apparently abandoned the idea.

At seven o'clock that third night, Kirsten was finishing up the dishes from the spaghetti she'd prepared for Garrett, Ross, J.D. and Matt.

Their talk had turned surly, enacting the behavior of men who'd come a long way for nothing, speculating as to whether she'd managed somehow to warn Burton Rawlings off contacting her again. Or to run.

Maybe he wasn't even in Seattle anymore. Maybe he'd bolted, slunk out of town. *And that would be her fault, now, wouldn't it?*

She'd snapped, "Oh yeah. That's what I did." No one blamed her; the talk was all for the sake of what was being heard across the street. Still, it grated on her, wearing her thin, making her feel frenzied inside, on edge all the time. Just that much more realistic. "You're right. I warned Burton Rawlings because his life is more important to me than getting my son back."

Standing at the sink, she understood well enough that the charade must be playing well across the street. By the talk they heard from the bugs Matt had planted, Loehman's henchmen believed, hook, line and sinker, that she was completely at the mercy of the precariously unstable nutcases from Tri-Cities. The kidnapping had fooled them.

They believed Garrett and his men were traitors to the cause, willing to do anything to gain the leverage necessary to wrest control of the TruthSayers from Chet Loehman.

But the situation was growing nasty. On the premise that Rawlings might try to approach her if she were alone, Garrett's team was considering the possibility of sending her looking. On the other side, the boys in the band contemplated rescuing her, believing that she was in fact holding out on Christo's kidnappers. That she'd give it up for them out of gratitude for saving her from the thugs holding her captive now.

She drained the dishwater, and scrubbed the stainless-steel sink to its less-than-sparkling best, thinking how dangerously clueless they were. If they "rescued" her, what did they think might become of Christo?

Garrett walked into the kitchen. Her heart began to thump. There was so much left unsaid between them, so many hours gone by the wayside, taken up with trying to find Burton Rawlings. She didn't know what to expect, but it wasn't that Garrett would come into her kitchen and make sure the switch was flipped so their conversation could be monitored by the vigilante cops across the street.

"You about done here?" He pulled milk out of the refrigerator. Draining the contents straight from the carton, he tossed the empty into the plastic-lined trash.

"That's disgusting."

"When I want your opinion, lady, I'll take the trouble to ask for it." But he winked at her and her heart squeezed tight with the image of Christo squinting both eyes in similar attempts to con her out of fussing at him. "Don't worry. Without a man around the house, your kid won't pick up crude habits like that."

Her chin went up, her heart squeezed tighter. Though his tone slapped her down—and unwittingly, all the harder because he was the man who belonged around the house—his smile invited her to lighten up. "You're wrong."

"Yeah? About what?"

She felt silly, making a case for crude habits. "My son doesn't need a man with bad behavior to emulate. He's perfectly capable of inventing his own."

Garrett grinned, that lopsided grown-up version of Christo's. "Like what?"

Her eyes searched his. She wouldn't be joking or sharing the smallest details with real kidnappers. "He belches just like any other little boy, he scoops raspberry jam straight out of the jar with his fingers, he—"

"But then, he's only four, right?" He made some distinctively appreciative male noise that could have been a chip-off-the-old-block pride in his son, if only he'd known.

"I want him back." Her eyes watered. Her head dipped uncertainly. She turned her attention back to wiping the counter. The oddly misplaced moment of shared intimacy vanished, and she was back to being a mother dealing with lunatics who'd kidnapped her child because the man to whom he belonged wasn't coming round to discussing it. "I want my son back."

"And I want Burton Rawlings," he returned, in his role again as well. He took the dishcloth from her hand. "I have to go to a meeting. You're coming with me. Get outta here and go do something with your face."

"What kind of meeting?"

"A meeting," he snapped. "If you needed to know more, I'd let you know. Go."

He followed her up the stairs and into the sink and vanity alcove of her room, flipping on the clock radio as he went by it. She stood, uncertain of what he was doing or why he'd followed. He pulled out a vanity drawer and began digging through her makeup, choosing a small compact of sage and forest green–colored eye shadow.

Flipping on the mirror lights, he rubbed his thumb over the powdery cake of color, then turning her face to the light, gently stroked the eye shadow to her cheek, applying it as well to the outer edges of her eye socket. When he was done, she saw that along with the illusion of tenderness for her, he'd created the one of an old bruise.

He stood behind her, too close. She refused to look into his eyes reflected in the mirror because the pleasure that had unfurled in her like some hothouse orchid at his touch, no matter how briefly or wholly contrived to blacken her eye, left her confused and frustrated.

She started to drag her brush through her hair. He reached around her and picked out a banana clip from a basket full of scrunchies and barrettes and clips of different sizes and handed it to her. Swaying ever so slightly to the love song coming from the radio, his lips so close to her ear that she felt his warm breath, he told her to put it in.

Heat flashed through her, lightning scorching a path down a grounding rod that was her nervous system. The words were so innocuous. Put it in the oven. Put it in the car, put it in the envelop, put it in the cupboard, put it in, put it in... Ten times a day, a hundred, anytime but this the words would only mean what they meant, barely noticed or unnoticed altogether.

But the meaning she took, the one that came to her first, last and shockingly fast, was another, fraught with a fierce intimacy, edged in desire, prickling with needs she'd forgotten ever having.

Their eyes met in the mirror and she became for that lone instant all woman again, a sexual creature, more than Christo's mother or the object of an evil man's pursuit. She was the woman to whom he'd been making love that night, and the awareness of that, out there between them now, changed everything.

She lifted her arms to gather up her hair, taking overlong, exposing her breasts beneath the rosy-pink sweater she wore to the gaze and hands, if he chose, of her baby's father.

He expelled a breath with such harshness, she knew the same desire was hard on him. His hands settled to her hips, his thumbs stroked up her sides toward the curve of her breasts. Her eyelids fluttered shut as a tension, a pleasure more keen than any she could ever recall thrummed through her.

She watched him watching his own large hands moving over her belly, moving ever so slightly down, coming together. Her womb clenched and the breath in her expired. Sensation between her thighs returned to her with a vengeance and heat flowed from her. Then his hands strayed up, under her sweater, up her bare torso to touch her breasts, and what she saw reflected in his eyes was the thirst of a dying man too long in a desert wasteland.

"Kirsten." His breath on her bare neck came hot and damp and harsh with an overwhelming frustration. He took his hands off her, backed a little way away. A very little.

Bereft of his touch, as lit up and deprived of satisfaction as he, she stared at him in the old mirror with splotches of its silver missing.

His voice too low to be picked up by surveillance, he croaked, "The hair clip, Kirsten."

She swallowed and pulled back her hair and planted the clip. He picked up the eye shadow and rubbed color onto the skin of her neck and throat to mimic proof of other abuses, then tossed the small compact back into her drawer. Turning abruptly away, he walked out of her room.

MATT GUILIANI CAME with them. Kirsten sat in the back of her own car.

On their way through the northern suburbs up I-95, safely away from the bugs in her house, the white van following at a distance of three or four car lengths, Garrett told her they were headed to what they believed to be a meeting of local TruthSayers. As in the park when she hadn't seen him coming, she could no longer recognize him for the man in her mirror.

"These are the members we've confirmed." He passed a file folder back to her. Inside it, by the light of passing street lamps she found candid shots of half a dozen men and a couple of women.

"The guy in the photo on top," he said, "runs the show—Derek Feder. When I got the call from Vorees that you were at the police station, I was undercover on a demolition site. The same guy runs that job. He'd decided after a couple of weeks that he and I were like-thinking men. He'd been hinting around about bringing me into the fold.''

"Do you need him as a way to Loehman now, after all this? Or is it just that you can't afford to blow your cover?"

"Partly. But there was some urgency about this meeting, Kirsten.''

"Everything's urgent now, isn't it?" Urgent kidnapping, urgent meetings, urgent needs left unfulfilled because there was no place for them among all the other urgent matters.

He looked at her in the rearview mirror. There could be no way for him to be certain of her meaning, but there it was, lingering between them in the dark.

"The point of all this," he said, switching lanes, squinting against the glare of oncoming headlights, "is that a stakeout on your house is not an isolated operation. It's in the service of a larger goal, which is what we're trying to uncover."

She understood this was the essence of being an undercover cop. Unending hours of tedium followed by bursts of urgent activity in the wake of connections searched for and unearthed where none were apparent. Wringing the significance from every piece of information no matter how inconsequential it seemed. Exploiting even the unlikely, most threadbare opportunities.

Garrett's lifeblood. Despite those skills, in his own regard, he couldn't add two and two together and come up with four. She couldn't spell it out to him. The sting of it, made worse by Matt's perception, wasn't going away.

"I don't understand why you want me with you."

"Ordinarily, I wouldn't." He gave her a rueful glance in the rearview mirror. "In this case, my own credibility is riding on it. This is my own cleverness coming back to bite me in the butt."

"I don't get it."

"In undercover ops, everything's at least half-improv. You never know, going in, how you're going to make yourself fit in, so you adjust. You have to have excuses in place that'll be tolerated if you have to take off. I knew that Feder had a 911 called in on him about a year ago for domestic violence, so my story was that my uppity wife had run off with my kids, and I was waiting to hear she'd been found."

"So if anyone needed you," she asked, "you could legitimately leave?"

"Exactly. I had to go retrieve the little wife to get my kids back. Now that I've supposedly got the little ingrate back in my clutches, I'm not quite ready to let her out of my sight again."

Kirsten made a face, understanding now why he'd made her look bruised and battered. "That's sickening." The caveman mentality turned her stomach. But the more subtle, chilling image besetting her was that Garrett had in fact been called away to a meeting with the mother of a son whose very existence had been kept from him.

Garrett was not the kind of man he'd led Feder to believe he was. She knew that. And whatever similarity she thought she saw to his cover story only reflected her own derelict state of mind. It wasn't the same thing at all as being his wife and stealing his children.

Except that in all the ways that counted, it was too nearly the same.

Garrett took the next exit off the highway, followed the street for a couple of miles, then turned right and right again, putting them into a middle-class neighborhood.

A porch light shone, lighting the house number. Garrett pulled to the curb one house beyond Feder's and parked.

"Show time. Remember, Kirsten, you're better off not having a thought in your head. You're scared, you're bullied, you've been slapped around. You probably won't need to say two words."

He opened the driver's door, got out and opened hers. Matt followed.

The bi-level house was in a newer subdivision of houses all in a row, every fourth design the same. Derek Feder opened the door to Garrett's knock. Holding open the glassed screen door, he took in the presence of a second man, Matt, then his oily gaze slid to Kirsten and meaningfully back to Garrett.

She disliked him on sight.

"Guess everything is back to normal, huh?" Feder said. "Little woman back at home." He backed inside to let them in, sticking out a hand to shake when Garrett introduced Matt as his brother. "Missed you at work, bub. Good thing you called in. I was beginning to think you'd skipped."

"With three weeks' pay coming?" Garrett joshed, gripping Feder's hand. "No way. Honey," he said to Kirsten, "this is the boss, Derek Feder. Derek, my wife—Kirsten."

"Mr. Feder." Garrett's *honey* made her feel like snarling. She transposed the impulse into a timid smile. Keeping her hands tucked into the pockets of her jacket, she refused the offer to take her coat. "Thanks all the same. I'm a little cold. I think I'll keep it."

"Suit yourself." Bestowing a comradely look on Garrett and Matt, Feder led the way into the lower-level family room. Four of the eleven men present were ones in Garrett's file photos, along with three other women.

Feder briefly introduced them around. Matt sat in a folding chair Feder's wife provided. Garrett took the end of the sofa, leaving Kirsten nowhere to sit but at his feet.

Feder called the meeting to order. She sat through an hour of those eleven earnest men, normal, working-class men talking about making the country safe again. She was doing her best to appear as if she hadn't a thought of her own in her head, the cowed, chastened little wife.

What made the men so scary, so dangerous, was that their goals weren't unreasonable or unworthy. Who could argue against safer city streets or an environment where children weren't murdering each other or their parents?

But then Garrett made the move she recognized instinctively he'd come here to make.

"You know what the real problem is, don't you?" he demanded. "It isn't the lowlifes you guys are talking about. It's the lawyers. Get rid of the mouthpieces, and we might have a chance. Old Shakespeare had it right. Wasn't it him said, 'Kill all the lawyers'?''

Feder jumped on it like a shot. ''Exactly. And speaking of lawyers,'' he said, pulling a folio from the plaid fabric pocket along the side of his lounger, ''here's one for the money.''

His coarse, ruddy features twisted unpleasantly as he sat staring at what appeared to Kirsten to be a handful of reprints, then looked up. ''I mean that literally, about the money.'' He took one and passed the rest. ''Keep a sharp eye out for this miserable excuse for a human being. Name's Rawlings, and there's a nice little price on his head.''

Bile stung her throat. She knew then what Garrett had been doing, why he was doing it and why he'd chosen the moment he had to touch her. He'd suspected all along that the urgency of this meeting arose from Loehman's need to neutralize Rawlings, but Garrett had grown weary of the swaggering and arrogant talk, and forced Feder to cut to the chase.

He should have warned her.

Chapter Nine

She shot up and ran, tripping over her own feet in her flight to the bathroom. Hurling herself into the small half bath, she shoved the door shut behind her.

Her insides heaved violently. She knew at some level that she'd blown it for Garrett and Matt, and she hated herself for coming so unglued over a bounty, a death sentence on Burton Rawlings. She was a professional, a veteran of vile, gruesome crime scenes, but that didn't stop the useless retching.

Garrett shoved into the bathroom, closed the door and sank onto the floor with her, pulling her roughly into his arms. "Kirsten, pull yourself together. Do you want these cretins to figure out that—"

"Don't," she uttered harshly, jerking away from him. "They're talking about *murder,* Garrett! They're—"

He shook her. She felt herself sinking fast, losing it all over again. "What did you think this was about? You *know* what this is. You've known it since you heard what you heard on Christo's monitor. Rawlings was always the worm."

She wanted to shriek at him. Could he really believe that knowing a thing at some guesswork level two or three times removed and seeing Burton's picture being passed around so every Tom, Dick and Harry Vigilante in greater Seattle would be gunning for him weren't two appallingly different things?

But Feder banged on the door at just that moment. "Everything copacetic in there?" He sounded far, far more suspicious than concerned, and she knew it was her fault.

Her eyes flew to Garrett's.

"Fine," he called, looking at her, urging her, imploring her silently to pull it together. "C'mon, Kirsten. You can do this," he murmured, suddenly gentle, tender. He stood, lifting her to her feet. "Just follow my lead, okay? You can do this. I know you can. Do it for Christo."

Gritting her teeth, she nodded, willing herself to do what she had to do to save the situation. If it could be saved at all. "Okay."

"That's my girl." For a brief instant, stroking her back, he cupped her head to his chest, then reached for the door, a slaphappy grin plastered on his face.

Feder stood outside the door, his ruddy complexion a mask of angry suspicion. "What the devil is going on here?"

Garrett shrugged. "No big deal. She's got some bug, is all."

Feder's mistrust transformed into something only slightly less malicious. "That right?" Still with his hand high on the frame blocking the door, he leaned back, craning his neck around and called out to the others. "You hear that, guys? She's got some bug is all. I know. Maybe we got a new little TruthSayer on the way." He looked hard at Kirsten. "That it? Another little baby for God and country?"

Garrett stiffened, still in character, ready to take the creep on over bullying his wife. Kirsten laid a hand on his biceps and conjured from God only knew where a look of confused innocence. "Mr. Feder," she asked, her voice childlike, "I...isn't that okay? Isn't that a good thing? A new...a new baby?"

He stared her down. Her eyes flooded. Her chin trembled, and though none of it came upon her for any reason Feder could have fathomed, by some grace, he bought into it.

"Aw, hell. Don't cry. Here, you come sit down." He exchanged looks with Garrett and backed off. "Sorry. You just gotta question something like that comin' out spur of the minute like this."

Garrett shoved the advantage hard. "I don't hold with anybody bullying my wife." He shouldered his way past the man, his arm around Kirsten as he guided her to his place on the sofa. Feder followed.

"Don't get yourself in a twist now. Come on."

"Don't tell me what to do, Feder," Garrett snapped.

Kirsten sat on the couch where Garrett had been. She sent an apologetic look around the room and saw Matt at the patio window, deep in conversation with one of the others.

Distracted from her now, Feder noticed the same thing immediately. "You two got something to say, say it to the group. There's no room for cowboys here."

Matt's partner in the side conversation, a spectacled nerdy little guy of five-four on a tall day, returned to his seat looking a little defiant. Matt stuck his hand in his breast pocket, pulled out a toothpick, peeled the paper wrap and stuck the splinter-shaped bit of cedar into his mouth. "Doesn't seem like that."

Feder glared. "What do you mean?"

"I mean, offering a bounty is...unlikely to encourage togetherness."

"The point, wiseacre, is to share whatever information any one of us has."

Matt traded looks with Garrett. "You seen this guy Rawlings? Anybody seen this guy?"

Amidst a lot of negative head-shaking, Feder fumed. "So you're leading the meeting now, is that it?"

Matt shrugged. "I got no interest in running the meeting. Just seemed like the natural question. What is the bounty, by the way?"

"A hundred G's."

Kirsten looked at Garrett, hoping the longing in her to get away from this house would be seen as hope that her man could bring home a hundred thousand dollars.

Garrett whistled softly. "That's a lot of money. What's this guy Rawlings up to?"

"Not important," Feder said, reasserting control. "Loehman wants him."

"So what went on in your little aside with the clerk," Garrett asked, pulling a U-turn away from the curb outside Feder's house.

"Funny you should put it that way," Matt answered, "since the guy is in fact a clerk."

"Let me guess. A fish vendor in the market."

Matt plucked the toothpick out of his mouth and rolled down Christo's window just far enough to pitch it out. "You know, Weisz, you are a real killjoy sometimes. How did you know that?"

Garrett tossed him a look. "That's why they pay me the big bucks. So what?"

"No, wait a minute. I want to know how you knew that. What did I miss?"

"The introductions, maybe?"

Matt shook his head sadly. "Here I thought it was your brilliant powers of deduction. How'd I miss that? Anyway, he's tucked away in some outdoor fish market downtown. He goes across the street to the alley for a smoke once in a while. Says he ran right into Rawlings just in the last week, coming out of the InterBank Building."

"You *must* be kidding!" Kirsten sat forward in the back seat. "Aren't you?"

"No. He's sure of it."

"We'll have to pay the bank a visit. See if Rawlings has an account there, money stashed, whatever."

"He may not even have been in the bank. There are several floors of private offices in that building."

"This isn't even possible," Kirsten protested. "How can you take a dozen random people out of a population of millions and one of them be certain he's seen Burton?"

Garrett pulled to a stop at a red light and closed his eyes, pinching the bridge of his nose. "That's why Loehman's operation is so hairy, Kirsten. The membership cuts across all incomes, all classes. It's the whole six-degrees-of-separation thing. Somebody always knows somebody else, and all it takes is one Judas. What did the fishmonger want?''

''He wanted to know—just in case he sees Rawlings again and manages to tail him—if I'd take Burton down and split the bounty.''

''So you want to be the one to follow up?'' Garrett asked, dismissing the rest.

''With the fish-market guy? I suppose I'm the obvious choice.'' With a dejected flourish Matt whipped out another toothpick. ''You're going to owe me big time.''

''Sure, well, I'll trade anytime. Chatting up a fishmonger for jackhammering my brains out.''

Matt smacked his lips around the toothpick. ''Well, maybe you don't owe me that much.''

WHEN THEY ARRIVED BACK at her house on Queen Anne Hill, J.D. waved them upstairs into the sound-protected study and handed Kirsten a fax from her friend Ginny. Below the cover page was a drawing Christo had done, stick figures with a mom holding hands with a kid holding hands with a dad...and a dog labeled Wag.

Kirsten took one look at Christo's drawing, handed it off to Guiliani, clamped her mouth shut and fled down the stairs, banging out the back door.

Garrett frowned, staring after her. ''I don't get it.''

Matt wouldn't spare a glance away. ''Mom, Dad, boy, dog. Seems pretty straightforward to me.''

Garrett glared right back at him, feeling about as clueless as he'd been about the baby monitor. He looked down at the drawing. The taller one in a skirt wasn't recognizable as Kirsten. The stick figures could just as easily be Ginny and Sam Wilder. "Aunt, uncle, boy, dog. Even more straightforward. What's your point?"

"The boy's in need of a dad, Weisz." Matt crossed his arms over his chest, speculating, "I'd bet a month's take-home this isn't the first time Kirsten's gotten that message."

He had never heard Matt Guiliani bet so much as a ten-spot on a football game. "What makes you so sure?"

His friend shrugged. "My dad was all I ever wanted." He paused. "You going to go after her or what?"

He wanted to snap back that he wasn't cut out to play hero to her damsel in distress. Certainly not the answer to all Kirsten McCourt's problems. Or Christo's. But he turned on his heel and followed Kirsten outside, ticked off at Guiliani for no good reason he could even imagine.

He found her huddled on the stone bench by the sundial in the backyard. She looked up at him, her eyes lingering, darting away. Moonlight bathed her face. His heart thumped awkwardly because he didn't know what to say to her. He should know.

He expected more of himself.

"I'm sorry. This must be hell for Christo, too."

Her eyes darted away. "He's fine, Garrett. He'll be fine."

"He's a great kid."

"He is."

"Guiliani thinks Christo's drawing means he's desperate for a dad."

Her head dipped low. "He fantasizes a lot."

Garrett nodded, a smile coming slowly, fantasies of his own coming to mind. Current ones, in which she was there with Christo, the two of them with him visiting Snow Dancer, but old ones, too. "When I was a kid I wanted to be a freedom fighter like my father."

"A freedom fighter?"

"That's what they called the people who took part in the resistance in Hungary."

Kirsten turned toward him. "Your father actually grew up there?"

Garrett nodded. "He was sixteen when the Russian tanks invaded Budapest. In 1956 his family was all killed, his sisters raped and then killed. I don't remember a time that I didn't fully understand the horror of it. Or that he was never going to get over it. Freedom from tyranny was…everything.

"But when I was Christo's age—and years older, I had stars in my eyes. My grandmother was an honest-to-God Gypsy, and Kryztov—" he said his father's name in that deeply respectful, guttural way "—was a real war hero, darting out in front of those tanks, lobbing Molotov cocktails.

"What I didn't get," he went on after a moment, "until after my father died was how the reality of his experience shaped me. He had this saying that even if a Hungarian gets into a revolving door after you, he'll come out ahead."

"Oh! Christo would love that!"

"Me, too. Made me think of a superhero. But when the tanks rolled in and crushed the spirit right out of the whole country, no one felt like that anymore. He found the feeling again in America, but I always knew, like I knew the sun was coming up tomorrow, that freedom could never be taken for granted. That it was up to me to pick up where Kryztov left off."

In a way, it felt to Garrett as if his whole life had been a preamble to this. To bringing Chet Loehman before a jury of his peers where he would be held accountable for his murders, defended by some dream-team battery of lawyers whose job it was to assure his right to a fair and complete hearing. Just one of the rights of free people that Loehman trampled.

Now it had only grown more personal for Garrett. He wanted to eliminate the threat of Chet Loehman and all the TruthSayers so he could give Kirsten back her son. It came as a bit of a shock to realize what he wanted was to have it all count for something. He may not be the answer to her problems, but he wanted to be.

He wanted to be her hero.

Her son's hero.

The word lingered in his mind, a dimly recalled echo, a fragment of memory to do with that night in the Mercury Club when he had come to Kirsten's rescue.

"Garrett, I need to tell you—"

"You don't owe me any explanations, Kirsten."

"Then you know...?"

"All I know, Kirsten, is that I'm falling in love with you."

"Garrett—" His name rode the crest of a small cry.

"Shh." He touched a finger to her lips, but it wasn't enough. His hand strayed to the silky spill of her hair and tears out of nowhere crept up on him for the staggering need to be a man with his woman, to touch her, to remember and rejoice and reenact the night five years ago when they made love and he knew beyond question that she was meant to be with him, and he with her.

He brought his lips to hers, just touching, just sensing, and thought his heart would explode.

He could feel her warm, halting breath, hear her excitement pulsing, smell the need as thick in her as it was in him. But when she took hold of his coat lapels and dragged herself up to him, to take that touch of their lips to a kiss where he knew no simple kiss had ever been, he felt such power as he'd never known before either.

Her power over him.

The hero in her.

To say he was falling in love with her was a lie. She was his hero and he was so far beyond gone as to make the falling a distant memory.

WITHIN A MINUTE of the bank opening the next morning, a time Garrett chose to avoid the possibility of running into the fish-market TruthSayer, with a hand to Kirsten's elbow, Garrett walked directly to the reception desk of the InterBank.

He flashed his badge. "We'd like to see the bank manager, Mr. Delahunt."

The young receptionist, who had not yet even put away her purse, picked up a phone and punched in a couple of numbers. "The police are here to see Mr. Delahunt. Is he there?" She listened a moment then hung up. She gave them directions to his office. "You can go up. It's the seventh floor."

An extremely tall, gangly man with a light complexion, pale goatee and nearly bald head, Delahunt stood waiting for them in his office doorway.

Garrett stuck out his hand. "I'm Garrett Weisz, Mr. Delahunt, and this is Kirsten McCourt. I appreciate your seeing us with no notice."

"No problem. Come on in." He led them in, and directed them to the chairs opposite his desk. "What can I do to help?"

"We're looking for this man." Garrett pulled out Kirsten's Identicomp likeness of Rawlings, unfolded it and slid it over the desk. "We don't know if he's a customer or an account holder, or if he holds a safe-deposit box here."

Eyeing the sheet of paper, Delahunt's eyebrow quirked up. "Or none of the above?"

"Or none of the above," Garrett conceded.

"His name is Burton Rawlings," Kirsten said, leaning forward in her chair. "We believe he came into the bank sometime in the last few days. Please. If you could help us—"

"Ms. McCourt, do you have any idea how many people go in and out of this bank every day of the week?"

"Look, Delahunt," Garrett interrupted. "I'll have

a subpoena delivered before the end of the day, if that's what it's going to take to get the information I need. But Rawlings is missing, his life is in danger and any information you can give us now might make the difference.''

Delahunt turned to his computer and tapped in the name, then clicked through several screens. ''He's not a checking-account holder...no savings account, no CDs...no outstanding loans. Let me see about any that might have been paid off.'' He went rapidly through several more screens. ''No. Nothing.''

Garrett scowled. ''What about a safe-deposit box?''

''Those names are confidential.''

''I'm looking for a yes or no.''

Delahunt gave a flinty look, then turned back to the computer. ''No. The name you're looking for isn't here. But you have to understand that at least a third of the safe-deposit boxes are under company or corporate names.''

''Aren't the names of individuals who represent corporations in the computer?''

''Yes. But in another format altogether. Individuals with designated access to the boxes fall under the corporate umbrella, so to speak, and for that, I will have to have a court order to produce. And no—'' he held up a hand, anticipating Garrett ''—even if you give me the names of corporate entities, I won't give you a yes or a no. Not without the paperwork.''

''What about beneficiaries, sir?'' Kirsten asked. ''What happens when someone dies who may be the only designated person for a corporation?''

"In that case, we would require a legal, notarized Certificate of Death."

"Suppose it was a dummy corporation," she persisted. "What if I'm the beneficiary but I don't know the number of the box or what name was used to lease it?"

Delahunt frowned. "You're talking a fairly complex set of circumstances. How do you even know such a box exists under that scenario?"

"Any number of ways," Garrett answered. "The point is, do you maintain a computer list of beneficiaries?"

"Not as such, no. But we encourage our leases to put the names of beneficiaries on the record. That is a searchable database, but again, I'm walking a thin line here."

"One more yes-or-no answer?" Garrett bargained. "Then I'll see that you get the subpoena."

"Under what authority? The receptionist mentioned the police—"

"The Office of the United States Attorney." Garrett pulled out his ID.

Delahunt studied the credentials and made a note of Garrett's name, then looked up, exhaling sharply. "All right. What yes-or-no question would that be?"

"Is Kirsten McCourt the beneficiary of any leased safe-deposit box in this bank, whether this branch or any other?"

"You're pushing it, Mr. Weisz."

"Lives are at stake, Mr. Delahunt. Including Ms. McCourt's."

Clearly disarmed by Garrett's aura of absolute

sincerity, Delahunt returned his hands to the keyboard. Inside of a minute, he said, "Kirsten McCourt is in fact the beneficiary of the contents of a box in this bank, in this building."

Something akin to dread filled her. "Am I allowed to look inside it?"

"No, ma'am, you are not. That would be a designee, which you are not."

Almost relieved, Kirsten said, "I'm grateful to you, Mr. Delahunt."

"You're welcome." But she could see that he was unwilling to look at her, almost as if she were already dead. He turned to Garrett. "I'll be expecting the appropriate paperwork."

"Sir, the U.S. Attorney's office is also grateful for your help, but if you would, there is something more."

"Mr. Weisz, I've given you as much as I can—"

"I understand. We'll deal later with the contents by subpoena. But I have reason to believe Ms. McCourt and I were followed into the bank." He paused, his forehead creasing. "We also believe that the individual following is vitally interested in whether Ms. McCourt walks out of this bank with the contents of that box."

"I can't allow you access—"

"That's exactly what I want the person following us to know."

"What, exactly, are you asking of me?"

"I need a look at your security cameras. If we can spot him, Kirsten and I will go to the desk at the safe and try getting access to the box. She'll be refused, she'll make a scene, you'll come down and patiently explain to us that she will not be allowed access. You call security and they'll escort us out."

Delahunt sighed heavily. "May I ask a question?"

"Wait," Kirsten interrupted, a shiver going through her body. "Garrett, I'm not sure this is a good idea. Then they will know there really is something here. Wouldn't it work better if Mr. Delahunt simply walks us out, apologizing for being unable to help?"

Garrett looked into her eyes. "Kirsten, they already know something exists. That it's here isn't going to change any of the dynamics at all—except that no one is going to believe you walked out of here with nothing in hand unless we somehow prove it—not with Christo's life at stake."

Worry made her hands restless, flighty. She clasped them tight to stop the small tremor. She had never felt more helpless or out of control of the events in her life. Thank God Christo was, in fact, safe. She had only her own life to worry about.

Garrett took her hands in his. "It buys us time, Kirsten. You're not expendable to them as long as whatever this is remains locked up in the safe-deposit box."

She straightened her backbone. "That's some comfort, isn't it?"

The question was not only rhetorical, but a facade, sheer grit. He smiled, his voice low, husky. "That's my girl." He turned back to Delahunt. "Do you still have a question?"

His complexion cast now in a grayish hue, the

bank manager shifted uneasily in his chair. "What is in that box?"

"We don't know."

"But if I'm reading you right, Ms. McCourt's life is nevertheless threatened unless this…this man following you can be convinced that she has not seen or acquired whatever is in the box?"

"Yes."

Kirsten shivered, hard.

Delahunt nodded, sneaking an unsettled, uneasy peek at a photo of his wife and children on the credenza behind his desk. Apparently decided, he stood. "Come with me."

He strode into the hall, then inserted a key into the call button on a private elevator concealed behind an ordinary office door. Kirsten walked ahead of Garrett and the manager into the small space. Delahunt explained that the elevator only stopped just outside the door of the vault on the first floor, and on the underground level where the security videocams were monitored.

They exited into the windowless offices of the security detail. The setup reminded Kirsten powerfully of the security area in the Federal Building, which had been Lane's domain. She waited while the bank manager explained the situation to the shift commander, who then directed them to the video monitors.

"There are twelve videocams in all for the inside of the lobby. Three more trained on the street outside and these, on the parking garage. Have a look. See if you can spot your man."

Garrett first searched the more highly mobile pop-

ulation on the street outside the bank, then the screen
of the videocam focused on the parking area where
they'd left Kirsten's car. The white van was
squeezed into a space just below the camera. "This
is it."

There was no one inside the van.

Kirsten meanwhile glanced from one to another
of the twelve monitors inside the lobby, searching
faces for one familiar from the boys in the band and
the Identicomps she'd done on them with Matt. She
spotted several possibilities, but when the techni-
cians zoomed in for her, none of them panned out.

Then a woman seated at a set of four monitors
stiffened. "That's the second time this guy has
moved to the back of the line. I think I saw him
earlier, too, filling out a deposit slip or something."

Garrett and Kirsten bent over the security tech's
shoulder. "Which line?"

In her own element now, Kirsten spotted him immediately. "This guy, right here." The tech nodded,
already zooming in. They had to wait a few seconds
until the guy turned a little more fully to the camera,
but when he had, Kirsten knew. "Garrett, he's the
one. He was wearing that same brown windbreaker
in the park."

"Yeah." He nodded grimly. "Okay. Delahunt?"

Though the bank manager had stood back a way,
he came close to get a look at the target audience
of their charade.

Kirsten asked, "Will the clerk at the vault desk
call you?"

He gave a brief shake of his head. "No. Not even
if you ask for me—which you wouldn't do, right?

Because, theoretically, I've already refused you, and your guy there may have been told by the front receptionist that the two of you were directed to my office. Protocol dictates that the vault clerk call security immediately."

Garrett asked Delahunt if he would alert the clerk to break with standard procedure and phone him first. "That way Kirsten will have the chance to protest. She won't want you to come because you've already turned her down, and that will be clear to this jerk following us."

Delahunt nodded. "All right." He took them back up in the security elevator. Garrett shook Delahunt's hand again, thanking him.

"Just do me a favor and deliver on the papers." Delahunt looked to Kirsten. "I'm sorry for your trouble, whatever it is. With this man on your side, you'll probably come out okay."

"Thank you."

Once they were in the public-access elevator Garrett muttered, "'Probably'? What's that?"

"The truth." She looked at him solemnly. "I haven't heard any guarantees out of you yet."

He stuck his hands in his pockets and looked down. A laugh finally bubbled out of her. "Lighten up, Weisz, or face the consequences."

"Which would be what?" The elevator dinged and the doors opened on the main-floor lobby.

"Having to call in the men in white coats, armed with syringes and straitjacket."

"Consider me enlightened."

She rolled her eyes. "Which way, oh Weisz one?"

He scowled and took hold of her elbow again guiding her toward the vault. "Our mark has just now spotted us. He's ducking out of line again, headed our way. Are you ready?"

It didn't matter whether she was or not. She had to play her role. The sixtyish vault clerk sat with a pleasant smile on her face. "How can I help you?"

"My name is Kirsten McCourt." She began to pull out her driver's license. The clerk gave no indication whatever of having heard her name before. "What ID do you need?"

"That'll be fine. What box are you accessing today?"

"I'm not sure. I'm listed on your beneficiary roster, though, so—"

"You don't have a key?"

"No. As I said, I'm a beneficiary."

"A death certificate, then?"

"No. I mean, not with me. But I need to get into the box today—"

"I'm afraid I can't help you, then. There are rules."

Kirsten let her voice rise, take on an edge. "I know there are rules, but you don't understand. I *need* into that box." She went on another few seconds, invoking Delahunt's name, implying he'd agreed to open the box due to her unusual circumstances.

"Well, miss, why don't I just call our manager and get confirmation of that—"

"No! I mean…"

The clerk was already dialing. Inside of a minute Delahunt appeared, flanked at the elevator door by a couple of security guards. Garrett made some comment about having warned her this wouldn't work. She stared angrily at him, then caught sight of the security team and behind them, a glimpse of the guy from the white van, wearing the brown windbreaker.

At the last second, Garrett veered from the scenario he'd invented. Jerking her around, he pulled her away with him and held up a hand to the security men. "Take it easy, guys. She's upset. She didn't mean to make a stink. I'll get her out of here right away."

Not satisfied with the offer to leave, one of them demanded ID, but Delahunt stepped in. "Let her go. I think Ms. McCourt understands she is not advancing her cause with this behavior. There is no way this bank is opening a box for inspection that does not belong to her."

Several feet away, grabbing up a fistful of bank flyers for some semblance of purpose in having been there at all, the guy in the windbreaker made a beeline for the revolving front doors.

Chapter Ten

Garrett pulled out of the InterBank parking garage into a tangle of early-morning business traffic. When he got to the highway, he turned in the direction of the demolition job site.

"I thought you were taking me home."

"I changed my mind." He first had to put in an appearance at the job, then convince Grenallo to go before some magistrate asking for the subpoena he'd promised Delahunt, based on hunches. He probably didn't have to do better than that, but it'd be nice. "Kirsten, do you have any idea what's in that box?"

"None," Kirsten said. "Burt was obviously on to something, but I can't even guess at what could provoke Loehman to all of this—and still not be enough for Burton to simply hand it over to Grenallo. I'd guess he still needed some kind of photographic authentication. He was hoping I could provide it. That's all I know."

"Any ideas on the subject matter?"

She struggled to remember anything Rawlings might have said that would give them a clue. "The thing is, Garrett, that I simply wasn't paying attention. I wasn't interested—no, that's not even right. It went beyond disinterest. I didn't want to know what he was doing. I think he picked up on that. I had the feeling just before he left my house that he'd made the decision not to tell me what he was really doing. Maybe even hoping to protect me.''

Garrett frowned. ''Too late, though. What about the first few times he called you?''

''He wanted to know if I'd kept anything of Lane's. Papers, records, any stored computer data, but I think even then he might have been worried about covering his tracks. He never came out and asked for something specific. Even if he had, I kept nothing Lane had ever even touched.''

Garrett signaled and crossed a couple of lanes in anticipation of the highway exit off I-95, then, at the last moment, when he saw that the white van trailing too far behind, was suddenly boxed in and unable to compensate, he veered off the interstate.

Unprepared for the wild ride, Kirsten grimaced and slammed a hand against the dash to brace herself, but then saw that he'd succeeded in shedding their tail.

Garrett didn't lose a beat. ''Start at the beginning then. Tell me what happened five years ago. How did things come apart?''

She'd tried to forget that as well, but those memories weren't ever going away. She took a deep breath to steady her nerves, then plunged in.

''Actually it started six years ago. Grenallo's team was pulling together the threads of an operation that had been going on for nine months or a year, even then. Some FBI guys had been undercover that long, infiltrating the TruthSayers organization. One of them had a fairly secluded ranch house that over several months' time became one of Loehman's favorite hangouts.''

"Was this in Montana?"

She shook her head. "Eastern Washington. Loehman was still moving around a lot. Anyway, Grenallo's team had managed to cut some access through the rafters and the dead space below the roof of this ranch house for surveillance. They'd called in a team of experts from the bureau to set up cameras and video, but the team was killed in that commuter plane that went down near Spokane. Do you remember hearing about that?"

"Yeah." They'd arrived at the demolition site. Garrett drove her car up over the curb behind other crew trucks. "I want you to sit here and look sick, okay? I'll be back in two minutes."

He got out and slammed the door, heading toward the job trailer. This act was going to be a little dicey, nothing he couldn't handle, but he had to play it so Feder believed he was the one calling the shots.

Feder was just coming out of the trailer. He glared at Garrett. "What do you think this is, Weisz, some banker's hours' job?"

He jerked a thumb at Kirsten's car. "Wife's still sick. I couldn't leave her at home. I don't trust her." He kept on trudging over the site strewn with concrete chunks that had fallen off the dump trucks.

"Where are your kids?" Feder demanded.

"My sister's got 'em."

"And you're just gonna let a pregnant woman sit there in the car all damned day?"

Not answering, Garrett shrugged and pulled the work gloves out of his coat pockets. He bent over and started working the combination lock on his toolbox. "Truth is, we can't afford any more lost time. Not and pay for her doctors."

"How many screws you got loose, Weisz? Wasn't it you lecturing me about women and kids? Get outta here. I'll spot you a couple of days' pay."

Feigning gratitude, Garrett closed his toolbox and walked off. Feder made some parting shot Garrett didn't hear over the sound of a wrecking ball. He stripped off his gloves, opened the car door, got in and jammed the clutch to the floor, peeling out.

Kirsten clung to the seat belt crossing her torso. "What did you tell him?"

"You're sick." He grinned. "Feder insisted I take the rest of the week off."

"You are shameless."

"One of my many outstanding qualifications for an undercover cop."

"Did you lay it on really thick?"

"Only as thick as it needed to be. What was he going to think, Kirsten? I was ready to go to work."

"But you weren't!"

"Well, see, that's where you're wrong. I'm always ready to do what I have to do."

"You mean you really would have let me sit here all day?"

"Of course not." He gave her a look. "Kirsten...I know how to play people, okay? It's what I do, and I'm good at it. I knew he'd buy it."

"But what if he hadn't?"

"Then I would have thought of something else. Could we get back to the story now?"

Shivering, she reached for the heater. "It's just so...false, I guess." She shrugged. "I don't know how you do it, is all."

"I just do what I have to do. So, what happened when that plane went down?"

She reoriented herself to where she'd left off. "I happened to be in Grenallo's office when he got the news. I was delivering some totally unrelated crime-scene graphics he'd asked for."

"Interesting coincidence."

"I'd been lobbying for a long time to get onto the investigative side, Garrett."

"But no experience outside of crime-scene work?"

"No. But they needed someone desperately. There were a couple of other cases taking up a lot of resources. Everyone else was assigned once Grenallo had a commitment from the FBI team."

"Okay, I'll buy that in the short term you may have been the only choice. But that operation went on for weeks, didn't it?"

"Grenallo was happy with what I was doing. He didn't have any reason to pull me off the case." She sounded a little defensive. "Is that so hard to believe?"

"No. I didn't mean to suggest that you weren't getting the job done. But you know Grenallo. Are you telling me you weren't surprised that he let you run with it?"

"No. I was shocked, really." She paused a moment, considering. "I made a believer out of him,

Garrett. When he saw what I was producing, he was happy enough.''

''What was it?''

''Hundreds of photos, at least twenty videotapes when they were edited. I had Loehman on film suborning perjury, ordering an execution, constructing an elaborate smear campaign against Senator Vogel—'' She hesitated, maybe seeing a flash of recognition on Garrett's face. ''Did you know him?''

He nodded. ''Margo was Ben Vogel's executive assistant.''

Kirsten fell silent.

''She was killed when Vogel's car went over the Aurora bridge. Vogel and the driver survived, but Vogel was left paralyzed.'' He looked at Kirsten. ''You knew that?''

She shook her head. ''No. But everyone expected Loehman to feel cheated. He'd devoted months working the smear campaign. He'd really rather have seen Vogel's career destroyed than the man pull out.''

Garrett dragged a hand through his hair. He knew Margo had been struggling with the fear that her own image was suffering by her association with Vogel, who was an honorable man, but badly flawed. Even then, Garrett realized now, he hadn't much liked Margo's attitude.

He pulled into parking a half mile short of the Federal Building. He needed the rest of it. They got out of the car, he locked the doors and they began walking.

''Okay. So in the end, you had Loehman on camera executing one of the men who'd turned on him.''

"Yes. It took almost a year, but we finally had enough."

Garrett drew her aside to a street vendor and bought a couple of cups of coffee, a Danish for himself, a poppy-seed muffin for Kirsten. They sat at a table beneath the cover of an umbrella to escape the constant drizzle.

He went to the subject of her husband. "When did you meet Lane Montgomery?"

"His company got the contract for the security of the Federal Building a couple of weeks after I was assigned to the undercover operation. We met almost immediately after that." She exhaled sharply. "I was such a fool. He was just so...I don't know. Earnest, I guess. So sweet." She swallowed hard. "Such a liar."

"Kirsten, you weren't the only one who fell for his line. He had to have impeccable credentials even to be in the running."

"I know that, Garrett. But I'm the one who married him. I had my evidence backed up and stored in half a dozen different places, but he was the security expert, and he knew where I had them all."

Garrett shook his head. "What makes a man in his position sell out to someone like Loehman?"

"I guess it's always about money."

Garrett gave her a look. His question had been rhetorical.

She shrugged. "In the end, either Loehman tried to stiff him the money he'd promised if Lane could make the case go away, or else Lane wanted more."

"Not necessarily. Montgomery was a loose end Loehman had to tie up in any case."

Kirsten's shoulders rounded down. "None of this leads us anywhere, Garrett. We have no more idea what's in that safe-deposit box than we did before."

"I'm sure what we've got is enough to get a subpoena. It would have been cleaner with something more substantial to go on, but Grenallo's office isn't going to be refused. Particularly since Rawlings was Montgomery's corporate counsel."

She finished her coffee. "I don't think I should be along when you ask Grenallo to go after the subpoena. I'll wait for you in the bookstore. Maybe try again to get through to Christo." For several hours she hadn't been able to get an answer on the cell phone Garrett had given Ginny and Sam. The weather reports were all bad. The northern Rocky Mountain region was socked in by the blizzard Garrett had just beaten getting Christo there.

Plagued by a fear that Loehman was somehow luring them all into some deadly ambush, she tried several times in the next hour and a half to reach the Wilders.

There was no answer.

Cut off from Christo, struggling to keep herself together, she took a little comfort from knowing that, as much as thwarting her, the blizzard insulated Christo all the more from the world in which Chet Loehman loomed so large.

NOT UNTIL the end of the day did they have their answer. Grenallo had gone before a magistrate, made his case, but failed to come away with the subpoena Garrett had believed to be all but a slam dunk.

It made no sense, only set them all on edge that any federal magistrate would refuse the petition. Garrett blamed himself. Grenallo had only shrugged. Loehman hadn't built his organization or remained a free man for so many years, through so many efforts to bring him down, without friends in high places, but to hear Grenallo intimating, even privately, that the judge was one of them, came as one nasty, disheartening blow.

As if that weren't bad enough, at 7:37 and 33 seconds, by the digital clock on the monitoring equipment J.D. was handling, the bugs Matt had planted across the street fell silent.

Matt responded by collecting the ones planted in her house, dumping them down the toilet.

The jig was up on both sides.

She could feel the tension of the men surrounding her ratcheting higher. They had no clue now as to what the boys in the band would attempt next. If they were acting under Loehman's orders, Matt believed, they would be closing up shop, and soon.

"Look," Matt reasoned, "they now know Kirsten tried and failed to get at whatever is in the InterBank vault. What's the point in waiting around for her to come into possession of the contents of that box if a federal magistrate is going to keep it out of her hands?"

"You're assuming," Garrett argued, "that they're convinced that what they've been waiting on is what's in that safe-deposit box."

"Yeah, and I'm betting they're better informed than we are."

"How could they be?" J.D. demanded. "We know what they know."

"Yeah?" Matt raised his eyebrows. "Well, we didn't know they'd found the bugs. It's possible they've been stringing us along."

"And we're right back to Loehman having invited us to this party in the first place." Garrett dropped a fist on the dining-room table and swore. "What the hell is he up to?"

"I think he's won this one, Garrett," Kirsten said. "Loehman really can't lose. He won't stop until he tracks Burton down. When that happens, if Loehman still doesn't get what he wants from him, then Burt's a dead man, and whatever he had comes to me as the beneficiary, and then—"

"No," J.D. answered, preventing her from going on, uttering the words anticipating her own demise. "Then he'll have to come through us and that isn't going to happen."

She shook her head. "He'll just wait. You'll see. If Loehman ordered Burt's murder tonight, the body wouldn't need to show up for months. He can afford to wait till you're not around anymore. You can't keep me on round-the-clock protection until Loehman decides to move, even if I could live like that."

Garrett sat both in awe and horror at her ability to reason as Loehman would. Perhaps it was all the weeks, all those years ago, of watching Loehman in action through the lenses of her cameras, hearing him plot and scheme, that gave her such a certain grip of Loehman's sheer cunning.

She was right. Dead right.

Even if Loehman made the expansive, foolish

gesture again of letting her live, all he would have to do under Kirsten's scenario was wait a few months and then arrange for Rawlings's body to be found and identified without any fanfare. Once a death certificate was signed by a coroner, Loehman had only to move on Kirsten, force her to produce the certificate at the bank to claim the contents of the safe-deposit box, and then walk out with the goods, whatever they were, scot-free one more time, but with at least one more death, one more coup counted on the impotent Office of the U.S. Attorney.

None of that mattered. Kirsten was the one standing between Loehman and whatever trouble Rawlings had managed to bring down, and Loehman wouldn't let her draw one breath beyond the last moment she was of any use to him.

"So what now?" Matt asked. "Keep Kirsten under guard until we can get someone to overturn the jerk and issue a subpoena?"

"It's a possibility. Probably the best one we've got at the moment," J.D. agreed, but his next words upset her. "If we could just lay our hands on Rawlings first, we might be able to pull this out."

"I hope he's gone." No matter what happened now, whether Burton Rawlings lived or died would have no effect on Loehman's plans for her. She got up from the table and began to clear away the accumulated debris of a couple of fast-food meals. Garrett followed her into the dark kitchen, and when she couldn't contain the tears of utter frustration any longer, pulled her away from cramming wrappers into the trash, and into his arms.

"Kirsten."

He wanted to promise her that this wasn't over yet, but even if he dared, what was the upside, when all she wanted, all she was fighting for, was that it be over? Her body came curiously still against his, and he didn't know whether to think she'd given up or was trying to absorb a little more strength. The hours of having gone without talking to Christo had worn too thin as well and she felt cold.

He held her tightly to him and rested his cheek on her head. She finally pulled back to look up into his eyes, but her focus went to his mouth and she lifted herself on tiptoe and brought her lips to meet his.

He thought of nothing but answering her in kind. She needed desperately to feel alive, to find some reason to believe she could go on, that she would make it out alive. The sound she made blistered his soul. Aware that in a heartbeat she would trade anything for one look at Christo, profoundly aware that the thought only made him love her more, he opened his mouth and covered hers, drawing her into a kiss so deep, so fierce and replete with meaning that he could no longer discern a separation of their souls.

She was all he knew, all he'd ever wanted, more woman than he'd ever had or known, still her own woman, still Christo's mother. And he was in love with her.

He deepened their kiss again and again to assuage what ache no kiss could begin to reach, when Kirsten stiffened and pulled back, burying her face against his chest, fighting to breathe normally. Behind her, a dark figure against the dining-room light, J.D. stood in the doorway, clearing his throat.

"Vorees just called. He's got Rawlings holed up in some dive down by the locks."

HE DROVE HARD through the pouring rain south toward the locks at the address Vorees had given J.D. Visibility was about as bad as it could get. The windshield wipers couldn't begin to keep up with the downpour. They reached the bar inside half an hour. By then she knew how Garrett wanted to play their meeting with Rawlings.

Vorees stood waiting, having a smoke beneath the tattered, mostly useless awning. Garrett let her out there, then sped around the corner to a parking place, reappearing in a few seconds.

"Is Rawlings alone?"

"Since he got here," Ross confirmed. "One of Ann's snitches found him. She's tied up so I tailed him here. Rawlings has been living in a rental at a trailer park about a half mile away."

"So he doesn't know he's been made?"

"No idea. You want me to stand sentry out here?"

Garrett nodded. "Get some backup to cover the back door, too."

Vorees pitched his cigarillo into the gutter. "You got it."

Garrett pulled open the door of the seedy Stowaway Tavern, and Kirsten walked in ahead of him. The place reeked of stale beer and faulty plumbing. She could barely see through the haze of smoke, or believe that Burton Rawlings would be caught dead in a place like this.

"Do you see him?" Garrett asked her.

She shook her head. "Not— Wait. There. Alone in the booth—"

Garrett spotted him as well. Taking her by the hand, he threaded his way through half a dozen tables to the bank of booths covered in faded orange vinyl. Burton sat alone, his back to what passed for a kitchen. If he'd been paying attention, he'd have seen them coming, but he wasn't.

Garrett nodded to her as they came within spitting distance.

"Burton?"

His head jerked up. "Kirsten...what are you doing—" His look was at first confused, and then when he realized Garrett was standing behind her, angry, finally turning gray with dread.

He made a move to get out of the booth. Garrett blocked his escape.

"W-who are you?" Rawlings sputtered.

"Possibly the only thing standing between you and extinction."

"Oh, geez, oh geez, Kirsten," he cried, his voice high-pitched, frantic. Clutching his head, he began pulling on his hair, moaning, "What have you done? If Loehman finds out you've gone to the cops—"

"Burton, he's not a cop." She swallowed hard. Tears filled her eyes, blurring her vision. "He's... Burton, listen to me, he's got Christo. They've taken Christo."

He cringed as if he'd been struck. "What does that mean, they've taken Christo?"

Garrett waved Kirsten into the booth opposite Rawlings and slid in beside her, leaving his back exposed. If Vorees hadn't been standing guard outside, he'd have been hard-pressed not to make Rawlings switch sides of the booth.

"It means, pal, that I've got the lady's kid. I want what you've got on your good friend and mine, Chet Loehman. What it really means is, when I get what I want, Kirsten here gets her kid back. And the way I hear it, you happen to be in possession of what I want."

Rawlings began to shake. He fumbled for a cigarette from a pack inside the breast pocket of his shirt, lit it and dragged deeply, repeatedly. He looked as if he'd aged fifteen years in the four days since he'd come to her house.

Whatever he'd been through had taken a terrible toll. She thought if he didn't get hold of himself, he was going to have a stroke and die. "Burton, you've got to calm down. You're going to kill yourself."

Already a dead man in his own mind, his look told her he thought calming down more than missed the point. "If you don't want to end up the same way, Kirsten," he uttered in defiance of Garrett, "then get the hell out. Get out now. The faster the better."

"That's not an option, Rawlings," Garrett warned softly. "Your friend, here, has her son to think of. Get a grip. Do it now."

So overwrought he could no longer think straight, he lashed out. "Or what? You'll take about ten seconds and then cram your fist down my throat?"

"Settle down, Rawlings," Garrett snapped. "If you'll get your head on straight, you might begin to realize we're on the same side here. I have zero interest in you. None.

"The *only* thing I give a tinker's damn about is getting Loehman out of my way. He's over the edge. He has no control, and if he goes on the way he has been all summer, the organization will break up and all that'll be left is a couple thousand useless, ineffectual, and frankly dangerous hotheads."

"Like you?" Rawlings spat. "Kidnapping innocent babies—"

"Burton, for God's sake, Christo—"

"Save it," Garrett cut Kirsten off, staring Rawlings down. "You've got no choice, and if you did, I can assure you, you'd take me over Loehman any day. For starters, my way, you hand over what I want, Loehman goes down, and you've bought yourself the chance to go on breathing."

Still shaking, Rawlings lit another cigarette from the first, then crushed out the butt and looked to Kirsten. "Have the bastards let you talk to Christo?"

She nodded. "I...yes."

"You believe him?" he asked, some part of him clearly desperate to believe he wasn't already a dead man, that there was still some chance, even if it meant aiding and abetting Loehman's competition. "You believe they're going to give him back?"

Despising her own deception, she had to remind herself that it was Burton Rawlings who had dragged her back into Loehman's deadly circle of influence in the first place.

"That's all that's left to either of us now, Burton. I have to believe it."

"Never pictured you consorting with the enemy."

"That's not how I look at it. I'm dealing for my

son's life. Unless I'm mistaken, you're fighting for yours.''

He dragged on his cigarette once more, then began slowly shaking his head. "I don't know. I—"

But Garrett had had it. Patience was its own virtue, more often paying a dividend than exacting a price, but his had expired. It had cost them days, hundreds of hours to run Rawlings to ground, and every hour that passed was one more tilting the balance in favor of Loehman figuring out that Christo was not kidnapped but hidden.

He reached across the table in a blur and grabbed Rawlings by the woolen scarf around his neck and twisted hard. Kirsten cried out but he ignored her.

"Listen to me, you sniveling little coward, and listen well. I've run out of patience, you're out of time. You either deal with me now, or your friend here will never see the kid again. Clear enough?'' Letting go of the scarf, he slammed Burton against the back of the booth. "Now what's it going to be?''

"Burton, please!" Kirsten pleaded. "What is it that Loehman wants enough to stalk you like this? What's in the safe-deposit box at InterBank?''

He stared, his mouth gaping. "How do you know about that?''

"We know," Garrett snapped. "What is it?''

Rawlings head shook so desperately he looked palsied. He took another cigarette out but didn't even try lighting it.

Chapter Eleven

"I...it's tapes, Kirsten."

"Tapes of what?"

"Evidence. Every last thing you had on him five years ago."

She felt the blood drain from her body. "Burton, what are you talking about? Are you saying there was tape backup of my personal files that I didn't know about? That no one knew about?"

"A variation on the theme, but yes."

"How is that possible, Burton? No one had access to those computer files but me. Hardly anyone even knew they existed. It was the first time that photographic evidence had ever even been compiled like that. It wasn't being done on the mainframe. My own computer wasn't even tied into the mainframe. No one could have—"

"Lane could, Kirsten." He lit his cigarette then. "And he did. From there, he made his own copies."

"Wait a minute. I don't get it." Garrett frowned. "You're talking about the same evidence that was destroyed by Montgomery five years ago?"

"Yes."

"And you have it?"

"Not exactly. It's a tape backup of Kirsten's personal files, but the photographic evidence on it is...inaccessible."

"Burton," Kirsten cried softly, frustrated, "what does that mean?"

"Computer security was our business edge, Kirsten."

"I know that, but—"

"I'm not sure you do." Resigned now, he began talking with more ease. "We provided the building security, but the reason Lane's company won the contracts for the Federal Building in the first place is that we were developing a system that had the ability to make computer data virtually invulnerable."

"Document security, then?" Garrett asked.

"Yes. We were way ahead of the curve. Absolutely unique. We were working out the kinks, but we were easily within six months of delivering the equivalent of an electronic notary service—a virtual guarantee that no data would ever be lost or fraudulently altered."

He gave a short barking laugh that grated on her spine. "If he hadn't gotten himself into financial straits, Lane would be alive today—and a billionaire. So would I." A violent shiver went through him. "Do you know how big a business this is, Kirsten? Any idea the amount of money to be made protecting computerized transactions—"

"Fortunes," Garrett broke in, cutting him off. "But if Lane Montgomery stood to make that kind of money—"

"Wait, please," Kirsten interrupted. "Burton, I really don't understand. Are you saying Chet Loehman knew Lane had backups?"

"Yes." His head tilting, he studied the orange glow at the tip of his cigarette. "Lane Montgomery's murder was never meant to be a warning to you, Kirsten. I started to tell you that the other night, and then—" He broke off, coughing. "You told me yourself Loehman never thought of you as that big a threat. He— Never mind. The point is, when I understood that's what you believed, I knew you didn't have any idea of what really happened. I knew there was no way you could help me, even if you wanted to."

"How could Loehman have known?"

He looked at Garrett, who answered her question. "Lane Montgomery must already have been in Loehman's back pocket."

Rawlings nodded. "Afterward, I guess, Lane must have thought he could go back to that well one more time. He had the evidence. All he had to do was blackmail Loehman—the tape backup in exchange for God knows what obscene amount of money. I don't think he quite grasped the implications of pulling off an extortion attempt against a man like Loehman who was more than capable of rubbing him out in the blink of an eye."

"I'm still confused about exactly what it was that Lane did," Kirsten said. "I had those photo files backed up myself. I even took tapes home so that they would be off-site. Lane had simple access to all of those. He could as easily have used one of those to conduct his blackmail. Why would he bother tying my computer into the mainframe?''

''You can never have too much backup, Kirsten. No one understood that better than Lane. But tape data can be copied over and over again. Loehman really had no choice but to get rid of Lane.''

Kirsten shook her head. ''I'm sorry, but Lane was smarter than that. Why would he take that kind of risk if the company was positioned to be worth billions?''

''I'm talking potential, Kirsten. Lane was already dead broke when he married you. No—'' he shook his head ''—that's not even right. The company was broke, and Lane was personally into the IRS for over a hundred grand. Probably ten times that amount to private investors. Meanwhile, Loehman was looking for the weak link in the evidence chain. Lane Montgomery was it, and you became the object of his affections the minute he appreciated the position you were in.''

Garrett took over. ''When did you find out about all of this?''

''From the minute I learned the evidence lockers had been destroyed. The next thing I knew, Lane was dead. I suspected that was what had happened, but I had no proof.''

Garrett didn't believe him. ''Just a nasty inkling, huh?''

Burton flushed in anger. ''Go to hell.''

''And that's what is locked up in a bank vault?''

''Yes.''

''Then...Lane paid the rent on a box in advance?'' Kirsten asked.

Rawlings nodded. ''That's exactly what he did—in the company name—actually a nonexistent subsidiary. The rent came due in June. With Lane dead, my name is the only one listed in the state's business records. The bank notified me, I went to see what was there.''

''Burton, was any of what you told me about the guys you met at that bar true?'' Kirsten asked.

Avoiding her eyes, he nodded. He looked at her then. ''I knew what you were thinking that night. That I was no match for Loehman. That I didn't have any business even talking to those goons.''

She felt teary again, sympathetic to his intentions. ''Burton—''

''No,'' he cut her off, refusing sympathy. ''I was stupid. They were… I'm sure they were probably laughing at me. But by then, I'd found that tape backup in the safe-deposit box, and it just infuriated me, Kirsten, knowing that evidence was sitting there, and Loehman was never going to pay.''

''But if that evidence survived, it would send Loehman to the electric chair. I'm sure John Grenallo would—''

''Kirsten, it's there, but it's not in any form that you can use. You see—''

''Come on, Rawlings,'' Garrett interrupted, impatient. ''What does that mean, 'not in any form that you can use'?''

''It's booby-trapped. That's the only reason I got Kirsten involved in the first place.'' He looked at her. ''You remember, Kirsten, the first time I called back in July? I asked if you had kept anything of

Lane's. If you'd ever found anything at all left with his handwriting. Remember?''

''Vaguely, Burton. But I'd walked away from all of that. I knew I didn't have anything, so I never gave it another thought. Did you ask me again?''

''No.'' Again, he averted his eyes.

Garrett swore softly. ''When did you know you'd already tipped your hand to Loehman?''

Burton's chin began to quiver. ''Not until...I don't know, weeks after that first call to Kirsten.''

She drew her coat more tightly around her body. ''I don't understand.''

''That first call to Kirsten,'' Garrett guessed. ''You must have said something about finding that tape backup?''

He nodded, his head wagging desperately again. ''I don't know what I said, exactly—''

''But whatever it was, Loehman understood the significance.''

''I didn't know that then,'' Burton protested.

It all came clear to her then. From Burton's first amateurish contacts with the two men in that bar, he'd been made by Loehman's people. He was watched, his house bugged, his phone lines tapped, which, all the way back to July, had implicated her as well.

There was no way he could have foreseen what was coming. ''Burton, when you say the tape data isn't accessible, that it's booby-trapped...what do you mean?''

He stubbed out his cigarette, croaking through the smoke in his throat. ''They're encoded with what I would call self-destruct instructions.''

"So that if they fell into the wrong hands..."

"Exactly. If you don't know the code, or if you aren't able to key it in within a very narrow window of time, the program not only refuses access, it destroys the data."

"So you were hoping the key was contained in Lane's effects?"

"Yeah."

"Aren't there hackers smart enough to bypass those kinds of safeguards?" Garrett asked.

"I talked to a guy who thought he might be able to dub the tape from one to another, minus the destruct codes, but I didn't want to take that gamble."

This was it, Kirsten thought. Loehman must have interpreted Burton's appearance at her house as a sign that the two of them had found a way to get at the evidence. The prize for which Loehman was prepared to do whatever it took to recover. Time never ran out on the charge of capital murder. "At least now we know exactly what Loehman is after."

"Yeah." Burton looked even more ill. Terrified. "Whatever else Loehman knows or doesn't, we're forcing him out of the woodwork. Clever."

"Burton, why didn't you go straight to Grenallo with this? He would— Burton?"

He was looking at her as if he no longer recognized her. "I gotta get out of here." He began to slide across the booth. Garrett straightened, his very posture a warning that they were far from done with him.

"I'm just going to the men's room. Look. You can see it from here."

Garrett sat back and Burton bolted for the rest

room. Shaking his head, Garrett called for coffee, three of them, black.

She didn't understand his look. "What?"

"'Men's room,'" he answered. "In a place like this, you hit the head, maybe the can. What you don't do is go to the men's room."

She looked down at her hands, then at Garrett. "Don't you think you're being a little hard on him?"

His jaw tightened. "He was a babe in the woods, Kirsten. The goons he met up with at the bar on the beach would have had him pegged inside of thirty seconds, and you ask if I'm being hard on him?"

Her eyes burned from all the smoke. At least that's what she told herself. "He was trying, Garrett. That's more than I can say for myself."

Watching the door of the rest room, he seemed not to hear her. "Yeah."

She took hold of his sleeve.

He tensed.

She thought he was overreacting to her touch, and took back her hand. "Would it hurt you to give him credit for that much? He must know he won't get another chan— Garrett? Garrett!"

He tore out of the booth blindingly fast. She screamed after him, "Garrett!"

But he was at the door of the rest room, his gun drawn, turned with his back to the corridor wall, aiming with both hands at the small crowd in the bar. "Everyone on the floor! *Now! Do it now!*"

A scream rose up inside her but her throat was frozen. She bent over low and crawled from the booth, trying to see, to understand.

She saw him still aiming, hollering now for Vorees, who burst through the front door with his gun pulled as well. It was about her, she realized, about protecting her. Still, she didn't understand. But in the instant Vorees was there to watch over her, Garrett turned and threw himself against the door Burton had gone through.

A cry tore loose from her. The force of his impact split the panels in the fraction of a second before the lock tore loose.

What he saw enraged Garrett and he swore, "Dammit to hell. Somebody get an ambulance. Vorees, cover me," and then he was gone, racing through the kitchen and out the back door.

Amid pandemonium, furniture, bar stools, chairs, tables crashing to the floor, the jukebox played on, some wildly obscene happy little Carpenters tune. Kirsten scrambled across the filthy floor, half crawling, half on her feet to get to Burton while Vorees returned fire aimed at her from outside the window beside the booth.

She heard Vorees shouting at her to get down, get to cover, but all she could think was to get to Burton.

She shoved hard, but Burton's body splayed awkwardly on the floor in the path of the door. She forced herself through the narrow opening and crouched beside him. Of the crime scenes she'd photographed, few were so benign as this. She'd imagined blood sprayed everywhere, but there was none save a small, widening pool on the worn, peeling linoleum near Burton's shoulder. Still, her stomach pitched and clenched and roiled again.

She clamped her teeth hard against the biting sour taste surging into her mouth. Feeling for the wound that was bleeding so profusely, she stanched the flow of Burton's bleeding carotid artery with her bare hand.

TRANSPORTED TO the emergency room in the ambulance with Burton, she held tight to his hand while the paramedics established an IV and ran fluids through a wide-open line. The van careened through streets inches deep in water, fishtailing nearly out of control countless times.

The ride could only have taken fifteen minutes. At its end, a crew met them at the E.R. entry. Burton was whisked out of sight, triaged and taken so quickly to surgery that he was gone before she got in the door.

In shock herself, so numbed she hadn't even realized she'd been grazed by a bullet at her upper arm, she sat through the ministrations of a physician's assistant under the harsh E.R. lights till Garrett strode in. The PA gave one last turn of a self-sticking wrap to her arm before Kirsten dropped over the side of the gurney and into Garrett's arms.

He held her for the few seconds she allowed. "They've taken Burton to surgery. I can't find out what's happening, they won't tell me, they—"

He looked to the exasperated PA. "I'm with the U.S. Attorney's office. The bullet wound is a critical witness. Is there any way you can find out what's going on?"

"I can call up there, but—"

"How about you *go* up there," Garrett asked softly. "I'd appreciate it."

"Well, sure. If you're here with her, I could run up. I just don't want to come back and find Ms. McCourt passed out."

"I'm with her. Go. Please."

The PA strode off, bypassing elevators for a set of stairs.

"Garrett." Kirsten felt suddenly light-headed, and sat down in the chair just outside her curtained area. "Did you catch whoever did this?"

His expression tight, he shook his head. "The area down there is a rat maze. There are uniforms covering the crime scene now, searching for the shooters. Vorees stayed to oversee everything, but I think our chances of finding them are nil."

"I don't understand how this could happen with Ross standing guard outside."

He knelt beside her. "The shooter must have sneaked down that two-foot alleyway between the bar and the body shop. He used a silencer, took aim through the window in the can. By the time Vorees knew what was going down, he was inside on my orders. It makes me mad, but...I can't fault the guy. Vorees probably saved your life."

Her lips pressed trembling together. "If Burton dies, it's because those bastards across the street knew that's what had to happen if I was ever going to get those tapes into my hands."

"Kirsten, he was a marked man. You know that."

"He could have been out of here a long time ago. He stayed, God knows why. He—" She couldn't get it out for the half-hysterical, erratic breathing that seized her.

The PA was back. "They're right in the middle of resecting your guy's carotid artery. The word is 'guarded.'"

"What does that mean?"

"Better than not. Ms. McCourt, I'd like to give you a shot of calming medicine."

"No. I…I'll be fine. I don't want anything."

"If you're refusing prescribed treatment, you'll have to sign yourself out of the E.R. against medical advice."

Her chin went up. "Show me the papers."

The PA looked to Garrett, who backed her decision. "I can't help you."

Kirsten signed the necessary papers, then the PA directed them to the operating-room waiting rooms. "The surgeons know you're waiting. They'll be out as soon as Mr. Rawlings is in recovery."

They were the only two present. All of the surgical suites were dark save the one where more than one doctor labored over Burton. Garrett paced the floor, talking urgently into his digital cell phone with how many people she didn't bother to keep track of.

She forced herself to sit still and drink a little hot chocolate. Another hour ticked by before a couple of exhausted surgeons in blue scrubs came through the pneumatic doors off the surgical suites. Garrett immediately closed up the cell phone.

"You're here with Mr. Rawlings?" one of the doctors said.

"Yes." He introduced himself, then Kirsten. "Is he going to make it?"

"At this point, I'm not optimistic," the older of the two doctors answered, "even barring any unforeseen developments. He lost a lot of blood, at least three liters, more than half his normal volume. We've transfused him and resected the artery but—"

"Can you bring him around?"

The surgeon looked hard at Garrett. "We could. It wouldn't be smart."

Garrett met, even exceeded, the surgeon's implacable look. "I need him conscious for thirty seconds."

"Garrett—"

He took Kirsten's hand and held it tight, but went on bending one more man in a long chain to his will. "Thirty seconds."

The doctor turned on his heel. "Come with me." He slapped the metal plate on the wall that operated the pneumatics, then turned toward the recovery room and gave the nurses the medication order to bring Burton completely out from under anesthesia. "You'll be damned lucky if he can answer even one question."

The nurse accessed a locked cabinet, came back with a small vial and syringe, then administered the medicine through a rubber port in Rawlings's IV line. Thirty seconds later, Burton came to, a tight, hideous pain gripping his features.

Garrett pushed Kirsten ahead of him. "Ask him, Kirsten, who's at the bottom of this."

Confused by the question herself, she turned to Burton and leaned over the gurney so he could see her. She took his hand. "Burton? Burton, it's Kirsten."

He blinked. "I'monna die, Kirs," he croaked.

"No you're not, Burton. You're not going to die. Please. Tell me if you can. Who's— Who did this?"

His eyes rolled to the back of his head, but he fought back long enough to utter the name. "'renallo." And one thing more. "Friends...very high...places."

Grenallo. The truth of it, the *sense* of it slammed into her. Now they knew why at every juncture in the journey to bring Loehman down, they'd been denied.

Right from the start, John Grenallo, the vaunted, respected acclaimed U.S. attorney himself stood above and behind the sabotage of everything Kirsten had sacrificed so much to do—and everything Garrett had done in the past four years. From the vantage point of knowing the truth, she could see clearly that Grenallo had supposed her ill equipped to handle the job he'd given her, and then when she delivered, he'd simply adjusted and done what was necessary to see her evidence destroyed. He'd used Lane, fired her and refused to take the case to trial over the protests of more than one of his subordinates.

She couldn't even imagine what tampering and obstructing he'd done to Garrett's operation over the years, but in the last twenty-four hours he'd not only failed to get a subpoena, he'd blamed the judge, implicating the magistrate in Loehman's collection of 'friends in high places.'

Garrett drove home without a word. The anger burned so deep.

She ran from the driveway through the house and up the stairs, lighting every candle in her room against the cold inside her. She stripped from her bloodied clothes, and stood under the scalding spray of her shower, shivering so violently she couldn't begin to relax. Ceaseless flashing images of careening through the streets in the pouring rain on a collision course with another murder tainted all the images of her life before, of Christo's life....

And of Garrett holding her only a few hours ago, their kiss, so inevitable, swamping her soul with hope of making everything right for Christo and his father at once, swamping her body with a dampening tide of desire...all of it interrupted, defiled by the specter of Burton Rawlings's life ebbing away.

One image bled into the next until finally it seemed as if Christo's life was slipping through her fingers, and all at once, she shattered.

Deep, wrenching sobs tore through her, and she sank to her knees in the claw-footed tub. She covered her face, trying to smother her own cries because she forgot the anonymous bastards weren't listening anymore and they shouldn't know they'd gotten to her, that they'd broken her.

She hardly knew when Garrett tore aside the striped shower curtain, twisted the wooden handles to stop the flow of water and sat on the edge of the tub. He bent over her and drew her naked and trembling into his arms.

Cradled as a child in a bath towel in his lap, she clung to him, burying her face against his shoulder as he held her close, his powerful arms surrounding her, his head bent low against her neck, uttering soft, deep, fiercely protective masculine sounds.

She wept as if it were the first time life had dealt her this kind of graceless, hideous blow.

It wasn't. But those times, ever her daddy's brave little scout, her tears were brief and contained, controlled and done and over with and a smile pasted back on her face before her heart had a chance to know the tears weren't done.

The images of Christo and kisses, the scent of a desperate, dying man and men who would murder and maim to protect themselves and their precious cause rose up again. The cry that came out of her was to her own ears the sound of something wild, trapped.

He shifted her in his lap until he could take her chin in his hand and turn her face up and bring his mouth down on her god-awful cries.

His kiss was nothing tender, but ravaged, fierce, aggressive, battling the darkness that threatened to eat her alive. She struggled against him like a woman drowning, certain of being dragged down, witlessly fighting the rescue. But he clutched her sopping hair in his hand and held her head tight and kissed her harder and deeper, dragging her up through the fathoms of torment, absorbing her ferocious protest until she broke free of the smothering darkness. He was her connection, the promise of her nightmare ending, her baby's father, and he became all there was, all she knew.

He rose, carrying her in his arms, turned and left behind the claw-footed tub and lay with her for an hour or more, molding his body to her shape beneath her blankets in the manner of pilgrims bundling.

He must have understood that there were no words to make it better or ease her anguish, and he held her against the darkness of night and the brutal hours, but though his warmth suffused her, she couldn't *be* warm, couldn't find her center, or the peaceable eye of the storm. She needed more, and somehow, he sensed that as well.

She turned in his arms and raised her head and naturally, his lips found hers. He groaned, uttered her name in a whisper so low, so close to her ear that it would otherwise have been impossible to hear. "Ah, Kirsten."

"Garrett..." Likewise, a whisper, unlike all the hours before, when she had first wanted to distance and protect herself, then later, instead, to reveal herself. To say aloud, *Garrett, my son is yours.* This time his name came naturally to her lips. And as if he'd been waiting to hear it, the sound of his name cut loose all his restraint.

He gathered her closer, his mouth covering hers, their kiss from his standpoint a barely understood echo of hello, from hers, a bid, a desperate invitation to recall that he truly *had* known her once in a sacred and biblical sense.

But even that powerfully unsated need in her gave way to his touch. Their mouths separating in only the smallest bursts for air, she clung to him and he turned on top of her, astride her, holding his weight on his forearms, kissing her forehead, her cheek, her neck, burrowing deeper, deeper as one candle after another guttered out.

One remained.

His tongue dampened her nape and the ridge of her collarbone, the hollow above and the tight, aching, sensitive areola of her nipple below.

Transported now in a torrent of emotion and remembrance, of the power of love and sex and life and birth, she arched into the caresses of his tongue on her breasts and his large, work-hardened hands at her hips, as his thumbs, roughened and hard, stroked her flesh and her belly across the span of her pelvis.

She clutched the fabric drawn taut against his powerful back and drew it upward and he raised to allow her to pull it over his arms and head, to release the fly of his button-down jeans and strip them away as well. But in all of that, still kissing and caressing, silent as sensual wraiths moving against one another, he managed somehow to apply to himself the thin layer of latex against all the risks of unprotected sex.

Of which Christo was one.

Even as her body craved his, even as every feather touch, every torching stroke, every kiss took her higher and higher into a tight and thrilling spiral, her heart sank deeper and deeper still into a morass of her own making.

In protecting them both even in the heat of passion, even in the pitched battle he waged to restore in her a shred of hope that love and life would finally prevail, even then he revealed himself as a man of honor.

He would not even have owned a condom the night of the day he buried his beloved wife.

Garrett Weisz was not a man to heedlessly spill his seed without another care.

Shame crowded in on her again, coming on top of all the horror of what had become of Burton Rawlings in that terrible, seedy run-down tavern.

While her body responded to wave upon wave of sensation and pleasure so deep inside that she felt her womb contracting, a tear seeped from her and coursed down her cheek. She'd intended none of what happened that night in the seventies disco of the Mercury or room 7054 of the Marquis, but she had gone to bed with a man she didn't know, knowing exactly what stand-in role she played.

She had Christo to show for it.

Garrett had only the dimmest recall, and still no notion that their union had resulted in Christo. Every hour that had passed, every time she'd let slip by her the smallest opening, made her silence in the hour before it just that much more unforgivable. It didn't matter that she'd had so little opportunity, or that she hadn't set aside her disappointment and taken the ones she'd had. Or even that the last time she'd tried, he'd been the one to silence her.

She had to tell him. He had to know now.

She stilled with him deep inside her body. Alarmed, he took her head between his hands. "Kirsten, what is it?"

She cupped his face in her hands. "It's Christo."

Chapter Twelve

But even then, she couldn't catch a break. Matt rapped on her bedroom door. "Garrett, man, I've got to talk to you."

"No, Garrett!" she pleaded turning his face, so filled with frustration, back to her. "Wait. Please. One—"

Guiliani's strained voice came equally imperative. "I'm not fooling around. This cannot wait."

"Kirsten, I'll be right back, I promise you—"

"Garrett—"

He looked straight into her eyes. "I promise you." He pulled away from her and jerked on his jeans, then went to the door. She covered herself with the sheet as he opened it. "What?"

Matt's hands balled into fists. Rage or tears glittered in his dark eyes. "Garrett...Kirsten—"

"Spit it out, Matt."

His jaw cocked sideways. "They've got Christo, Garrett. The bastards have snatched your son...Christo from the Wilders."

Garrett turned away, a physical pain racking his body, to Kirsten, whose tears and cry of anguish ripped a hole in his suddenly alert, suddenly stone-cold heart.

"My son?"

"Garrett—" Matt tried to get his attention.

"*My* son? Kirsten?"

Clutching the sheet to her breasts, she cried, "I tried to tell you...so many times, Garrett, but—"

Matt interrupted her, his voice low, urgent. "Loehman's waiting on the phone."

Garrett turned on him. "*You* knew Christo was mine? She told *you*—"

Matt swore harshly, toe to toe with him. "No one told me, Weisz. What did you want? A diagram? A calendar tattooed on your eyelids? Baby makes three, *paisan*, in nine, and if you didn't have your head up your—"

"Matt, don't!" Kirsten cried, scrambling off the bed, dragging the sheet along to cover herself. She touched his bare shoulder, pleading with him, stroking his stubbled implacable jaw. "Garrett—" He turned to her. His lips and chin trembled. Her heart cleaved in two. "I'm sorry. I should have told you days ago. I'm sorry."

And he knew he should have known, but he couldn't make his heart feel any less betrayed. He cupped the nape of her neck and drew her to him, cradling her to his so recently fevered body, her head to his chest, and prayed that he'd get over it.

HE PULLED his shirt on over his head as he flew down the stairs, about to do what he had to do in a fog of elation corrupted by a terrible anger at himself.

Unlike his father before him, he was not so harsh a man, but his judgment fell hard. Not on Kirsten for the secret she'd kept from him, so much as against himself for the truth he'd failed to discern.

He had a son. A child of his loins in the hands of his enemy. He didn't blame Kirsten for her silence but he couldn't tell her that or tell her why.

He hurt too much.

He believed, like his father, that a man's life always reflected back at him exactly what he deserved, nothing less, nothing more. Kryztov Weisz, dinosaur and Hungarian freedom fighter that he was, had taught his son that lesson as well, for it may have been the Soviet boot crushing his family, but it was a nation cowering too long.

A people who went along like lambs to the slaughter refusing to see the danger until it was too late *became* lambs to the slaughter.

Just so. A thing was what it was. The truth couldn't be any plainer, or the consequences of hiding from it any more devastating.

And when a man became a father in doing what Garrett had done, who would take a woman to bed and refuse to look back when he knew better, when in his soul he had recognized her for the woman he would want for the mother of his children, when a man so dishonored a woman, he had no recourse with her, no right to rant and rave about the lost years of his baby's life.

Just so.

But he drew the line at the kidnapping of his innocent son, so he got on the speakerphone with the man he wanted to strangle with his bare hands and began bargaining.

"This is Garrett Weisz."

"Mr. Weisz. A pleasure. My regards to the lovely Kirsten."

Sitting on the landing of the staircase listening to Loehman on the speaker, Kirsten clenched her teeth.

Garrett all but snarled. "Where is Christo McCourt?"

"I understand that the child is safe. I sympathize with his mother's concern, but you understand, what happens now is in your hands." He made no overt threats, no claim of possession, no admission, hardly a veiled warning.

Nevertheless, both sides knew Christo was not where he should be.

Temporarily distracted as Ross Vorees came through the front door, Garrett looked long at Kirsten as she sat on the stairs. What stood between them paled in comparison to what he must accomplish now. "What do you want?"

Loehman's voice took an unpleasant turn. "You know what I want."

"We don't have the tapes."

"Well, you see, that's the point."

"Of Rawlings's murder?"

Kirsten gasped at Garrett's tone with Loehman, the depth of his anger. There was no other way she could come to have the tapes in her possession save by Burton Rawlings's death. Loehman must have clearly understood that it would all be very much out of her hands should the tapes go into evidence via court-ordered subpoena.

Loehman was obviously unwilling to depend on Grenallo's intervention again. Rawlings had to die for the evidence to fall to Kirsten. And Christo was not only Loehman's ace in the hole, but insurance against the FBI being called in. Loehman knew whom he was dealing with in Garrett, thanks to Grenallo, who must also have given him the location where Christo had been taken for safety's sake.

Swallowing hard, huddled on the stairs in leggings and a sweater, Kirsten fought off the tremble, the overwhelming pall on her spirit, the desperation. Her faith, her only hope, resided with Garrett, whose stake was now so personal.

Loehman's silence grew overly long, ominous at Garrett's reference to Rawlings. "You should really avoid inflammatory statements like that, Mr. Weisz."

"I repeat," he snapped, "we don't have the tapes. You have my word—"

"Your word. I am impressed, I must say, but unmoved. I want those tapes."

"Look, Loehman. They're booby-trapped. They'll self-destruct. They're useless to anyone. Montgomery was the only one who could access them—"

"For the time being, perhaps. But you see, I've no doubt technology will overcome those problems. I want them before that becomes a possibility."

"You don't have to do this, Loehman. Turn Christo McCourt back to the Wilders. Let this be over."

Loehman wasn't dealing. "You have eighteen hours."

"That's not nearly enough time to—"

"It's the only time you're getting. As it is, I have to trust that you will have no time to tamper with the tapes."

Garrett exhaled. "All right. On the other hand," he bargained, "you'll be there to take possession of the tapes, or it won't happen."

"*Don't* dictate to me, Weisz. You will turn the tapes over to whomever I choose…"

"No."

"*No?* Have you lost your ever-loving mind? I just told you—"

"I heard you," Garrett interrupted. "Now you listen to me. You may have half of law enforcement up to and including the U.S. attorney in your back pocket, but there are traitors at the heart of your operation itching for the chance to leverage you out of control. I'm not going to risk the safety of that child by handing the tapes over to anyone but you. No one, Loehman. Rely on it," he commanded, echoing Loehman's own words.

"Fine. I'll be there."

"Where?"

"Get to Jackson. We'll talk then."

J.D. indicated he had a fix from the satellite tracking on Loehman's current location within a hundred-mile radius of Kalispell, Montana.

"Neutral ground, then," Garrett asked, to confirm that Christo had not been taken several hundred miles back up into Montana as well.

"Neutral ground," Loehman agreed. "The clock is ticking. Your time remaining is seventeen hours, fifty-seven minutes. We all know exactly what is at stake on both sides. Please do not make the idiotic mistake of calling in the FBI. Goodbye.''

"Before I move," Garrett asked before Loehman could hang up and kill the connection, ''tell me how Kirsten can talk to her son.''

All they heard was a cold, distant laugh and the click of a disconnect.

J.D. stabbed buttons on his monitoring equipment, calling for confirmation of his fix on Loehman's location.

Vorees was already on his cell phone, calling in sick to the detective bureau and arranging the rental of a four-wheel-drive vehicle. ''Somebody should go on ahead. I think it should be me. To be honest, I'm the only one they really don't know. With a little luck on the roads, I'll be a few hours ahead of you to scope things out.''

Nodding his approval, Garrett rattled off several things for Vorees to check out when he got near the Wyoming border. ''Keep a low profile.''

Vorees left. Kirsten rose from the spot where Christo launched his Indian raids and went down the stairs. Her face was still tear-stained, tight with strain. She went to her dark kitchen for a modicum of privacy with Garrett. He followed.

She stood with him in the dark, unable to see his eyes, making no excuses, dealing with the moment. ''Garrett...I don't like this. Why won't he let me talk to Christo?''

He made himself face her, look at her, *see* the woman he had left with child. ''He's still in Montana. Nowhere near Christo, and even if he were, he really doesn't give a damn if you get to talk to Christo or not."

Her eyes were dry, her tears spent. "What are we going to do?"

"We're going to get a death certificate—"

"But Burton is hanging on! We can't—"

"I can. I will." He looked at her. He would do what he had to do. A bogus death certificate wasn't a big deal. "It won't be the first time, Kirsten."

"What about the FBI? Aren't you supposed to alert them?"

"Yeah. And I would, if I thought it wouldn't get right back to Grenallo. He's dirty, and—" He didn't have to tell her that. He broke off, dragging a hand through his hair, frustration coursing through him on so many levels.

"What can I do?"

Tell me why, he thought. Tell me why. But what he said was, "Pack some warm clothes. Get some sleep."

She nodded. "I want to bring my camera. I need to go by my school and get my laptop with the right enhancement software—"

"Forget it, Kirsten." It wasn't for the sake of posterity that she wanted her camera, which meant she thought she was somehow going to be in on Christo's rescue, snapping off shots of the bad guys in action at the same time. "*I'm* not even thinking beyond getting Christo back, and then, the FBI can have it. I'm not going to have you—"

"Don't go there," she warned fiercely. "Don't even think of telling me I can't be a part of this."

"Kirsten, I don't want to argue with you."

"Then don't. Christo is my son, and this is what I do. It's all I can do." She bit her lip, her voice wavered. "Please don't shut me out. Don't take that away from me, Garrett."

Swearing an oath, his voice went gravel-like so he couldn't utter what was in his heart, couldn't correct her. *Our son, Kirsten.*

Ours.

His throat felt as thick as the worst of the channel fog. "I'm not trying to punish you, Kirsten."

"Aren't you?"

Was he? Didn't he want to know, didn't he want his answers, didn't he resent her as much as himself?

"I'm sorry. Maybe someday we can forgive each other." He touched her cheek. An awkwardness sprang up between them, a keen memory of what'd they'd been to each other less than an hour before, what powerful emotions, what intimacy, what she'd been about to say to him. How much was left unsaid, how much must be put aside until Christo was rescued.

He swallowed. Looking at her, he knew he could not explain himself, not in ten minutes, not in as many hours. He blamed them both, and loved her more, but in the dark of her kitchen with the scent of lovemaking lingering on them still, he knew that what he had missed of Christo's life was what made him want to lash out at her.

He didn't have ten hours, didn't have one to spare. He wanted to reassure her that he would get over wanting in some dank corner of his soul to punish her, but he didn't know if that was true and didn't know what else to say.

He told her to bring whatever she wanted and left her standing in the dark because he couldn't touch her either. Not and still keep to the shadow of a prayer that he would be able to return his son to his mother.

BY 5:00 A.M., four hours into their allotted eighteen, he had called in every favor ever owed him to get them onto a private plane that would make a landing near the Idaho-Wyoming border if it had to be made on an iced-over stretch of deserted highway.

By six-thirty J.D. had secured the cooperation of the hospital in releasing to the press the death notification of the shooting victim, one Burton Rawlings. Rawlings was not readmitted under an alias, but stashed instead in a private VIP suite.

At 8:00 a.m., Kirsten walked into the InterBank revolving door, through the lobby to the vault area where she presented the clerk with Rawlings's notarized death certificate, and the box, inside the vault lined with locked boxes, was opened to her. She removed all five tapes, which bore the identifying labels and codes Lane Montgomery had printed on them himself.

And at 9:00 a.m., Kirsten boarded the Gulfstream ahead of Garrett, J.D., Matt and Ann Calder, who'd called in to the detective bureau, like Vorees, and taken a three-day personal leave.

Two hours into the flight, curled up in her seat, Kirsten gave up trying to sleep. For several hours she'd had no time to think or worry, but now she couldn't stop imagining what terrors Christo must be enduring while the hours and minutes of her life marched relentlessly on in so ordinary a fashion.

She still breathed. Her heart still beat. Her thoughts still strayed to things like leaving a note for the milkman and putting out the trash. Things like needing desperately to know what Garrett meant by "someday," and what he needed her forgiveness for.

Christo was missing, stolen from Ginny and Sam with such apparent ease that Kirsten would never feel completely safe again, even if his rescue or ransom or return went without flaw.

Ann Calder appeared and sat down beside her. "Are you all right?"

She nodded wearily. Everyone aboard knew that this mission was personal now for Garrett as well as for her, but from Ann she felt none of the tension radiating off the men, only a quiet empathy she couldn't explain. "What about you?"

She stared out the window, at sunlight glinting off the clouds at thirty-some thousand feet. "I had a son, too, Kirsten." Her eyes glittered. "A baby born out of wedlock. I haven't seen him since the hour he was born."

"Oh, Ann. I'm sorry. What happened?"

"I had to walk away from him."

"My God, why?"

Ann let go a shaky breath. "It's a long story. When this is all over—" She broke off. "I don't know why I thought it would help to tell you that. It's just that from the first time we met, I've had this feeling that my life is on the brink of the same kind of collision course as yours."

She couldn't imagine what circumstances had made Ann Calder leave a child behind, but in some indefinable sense, having another woman around who knew what it was to grieve a child unnaturally missing from her life brought Kirsten the comfort of being less alone.

"Ann, I'm so sorry." She looked at the woman who had so quickly become a friend. She'd watched J.D. when he spoke with Ann on the phone, watched Ann watching him in the few times over the course of the last three days when they happened to be together under her roof. She thought there was something happening between them. "Does J.D. know?"

Ann shook her head, color staining her cheeks. "No one knows, Kirsten. You're the first person I've ever breathed a word of it to." A bewildered expression flitted over her finely honed features. "I thought I was done dealing with the loss of it. It's been fifteen years...I'm not sure J.D. would understand." She breathed deeply, composing herself. "Anyway, I just wanted you to know I share your feelings." She angled her head toward the men who were sitting in a tight little knot strategizing. "Actually, they sent me back here to get you so Garrett can fill you in on what's been decided in the last hour or so."

Kirsten took her hand and squeezed it. "Thank you. Your confiding in me means a lot."

Ann nodded. "You're welcome. But we'd better head up there now."

Matt moved out of his seat, which faced Garrett's, when she came forward with Ann. Garrett went right into it. "By the time we get to Jackson, we'll have six hours before Loehman's deadline. Word is that the roads are passable in and around Jackson now. We don't know what kind of place he's going to dictate for the handoff, or even if Christo will be there. Best guess is that he won't be. They'll hold him at some other location.

"Our goal is to find Christo and get him back before the time is up, but whether we have him back or not, we'll go through with handing over the tapes."

Reading between the lines, Kirsten nodded. It was unlikely that they would find Christo far enough in advance to make any real difference, and God only knew what hell Loehman would unleash if the tapes were not handed over to him. She'd heard them talking over the possibility of paging Garrett the minute they retrieved Christo, assuming it could be done in advance, but the point was really academic. They would have to go through with the handoff.

"Matt's been in contact with a local—a retired CIA analyst who was a satellite and telecommunications guru," Garrett said. "He's working on breaking into Loehman's communications loop. Matt will join him and work on pinpointing their locations—"

"And where Christo is being held?" Kirsten asked.

"Yes." He looked at her, a warning to keep her expectations in line. He took her hands. "It's a long shot, but we're playing it. If we get a break, you and J.D. will go after Christo."

She swallowed hard. "I thought you would want—"

"To be the one to rescue Christo?"

Exhaustion was taking a steep toll on her emotions. All she could do was to nod.

"Loehman expects me to hand over the tapes to him personally. I don't want to hand him any excuse to call off returning Christo." His look, though, told her he would have sacrificed almost anything to be the one to rescue his son. "We have to do this smart."

"I grew up in Colorado, Kirsten," J.D. offered, his voice low, gentle. "Telluride. Same kind of snow and terrain. That might give us an edge. Christo will need you. Vorees will ride shotgun with Garrett, make the handoff with Loehman."

She saw the logic in their choices. "What if we can't find Christo first?"

A grimace tightened Garrett's mouth. "Loehman and I won't be parting company until I know Christo is back with you, and that you're both safe."

THEY WERE MET at the plane by Ross Vorees, who had arrived while they were taking off out of Seattle. He drove them to Sam and Ginny's place, explaining that he'd spent his time without any luck canvasing motels for anyone checking in with a child of Christo's size.

Which, Kirsten thought, bundled into the back seat of the Suburban, didn't rule out motels because Christo was small enough to be carried in a large tote if that's what it took to keep him hidden from sight.

Garrett was making the same point when Vorees crested the hill and Sam and Ginny's mountain cabin came into view with six hours and fifteen minutes left to them.

Exchanging tearful hugs with Ginny at the door, Kirsten went inside and asked right away to go to Christo's room. She sank to the bed from which he'd been taken. Garrett examined the window with Sam where a hole had been cut in the glass large enough to reach a gloved hand through to unlock the window. Scuff marks on the freshly painted sill remained where the kidnapper had come in and taken Christo back out through the window.

Matt sat on Christo's bed beside Kirsten, reading the dog a riot act. "Wag is no guard dog, but I can't believe he wasn't at least barking at the kidnappers."

"He may have barked his head off, but Gin and I had him out front with us while we were hauling in firewood. Wag pretty much sat on the porch, doesn't like snow at all." Sam shook his head, his eyes watering. "I cannot believe this happened. I swear, Ginny and I—"

Clapping Sam on the shoulder, Garrett cut him off. "No one could have predicted this, Sam, or guarded against it. There's no point in blaming yourselves. Let's just concentrate on finding where they've taken Christo."

"That isn't going to be easy." Given something practical to do, Sam led the way downstairs to the dining room. He pulled a set of car keys out of his coat pocket and handed them to Matt, who was going off to work on the satellite surveillance with the retired CIA spook.

On the table were maps of every variety from USGS topographical maps to satellite photos of various magnifications.

Sam pointed to the one in which every building within a hundred-mile radius of Jackson could be seen.

J.D. grimaced. "A lot of rugged ground to cover."

"You're right about that," Sam said. "Trouble is, with all this snow, the lay of the land is masked."

"Where are we?" Kirsten asked. The only way she was going to get through this was to focus hard on the details. "Your house, I mean—on the map?"

Sam stabbed a finger at a barely visible rooftop a half centimeter south of the town of Jackson. "Here. Right here. See the road?"

She nodded. "They didn't use this road, though, did they?"

Sam gritted his teeth. "If they did, Kirsten, the tracks were wiped out when the snowplows got through."

"I thought you plowed the road."

"I do—the five hundred yards closest to the house. That I know for sure hadn't been disturbed, which means they didn't get closer to the house than half a mile with any vehicle other than, possibly, a snowmobile."

Garrett took a swallow of coffee. "It's dead silent out here, Sam. Wouldn't you have heard a snowmobile engine?"

Sam shrugged. "It's quiet now, but the wind was

blowing like hell. Howling around the house. I'm not sure we would have heard the engine of a 777."

"With all this snow," J.D. put in, "I can tell you right now these guys would have had this kidnapping planned down to the smallest detail. Nothing left to chance. On foot, on skis partway, maybe a snowmobile on the far end. They probably would not have made a lot of progress. Supposing they haven't taken Christo out of the area, we're close."

"If Loehman can be believed," Kirsten said, wanting badly to believe J.D.'s assessment.

Garrett looked at her. "Loehman wants those tapes too much to play games. We have to go with it, Kirsten."

She nodded. "How far is 'close,' J.D., in your estimation?"

"In this kind of weather, over mountainous terrain, no more than ten or fifteen miles at the outside."

"Well, that certainly narrows the search." Staring at the satellite photo, Garrett frowned. "It's a start, I guess."

J.D. shrugged, sharing Garrett's frustration. "Not much of one," he answered. "But if they approached the rear of the house where Christo's window is, and went back the same way, the incline due north was working against a man on snowshoes or cross-country skis."

J.D. got deeply into a series of possible scenarios. Too tense and unfamiliar with the mountains or lingo to follow his explanations, Kirsten wandered into the kitchen. Ginny followed and poured her a cup of Earl Grey tea, but her cup rattled as she set in down on the saucer after only one sip.

"Kirsten, what's going on?"

She straightened. Nothing got by Ginny, ever had or ever would. One overlong look between them was sufficient to arrest her best friend's attention. "Garrett Weisz is Christo's father."

Ginny blinked. "I don't think I heard you—"

She gave a bittersweet smile. "Small world, isn't it?"

"Small world?" Ginny asked, incredulous. "Kirsten, I don't believe you. Did you know who he was all along? All this time? Was he someone you knew from when you were on the task force? Is he married, is that why—"

"Ginny, no! It's nothing like that. I've never lied to you."

"That's not exactly true."

"What I mean is, nothing I finally told you was a lie. We *were* strangers to each other. Five years ago Garrett Weisz was in the military, winding up his last tour of duty in naval intelligence. He was based in Seattle, but I— He had nothing to do with the task force I was on."

Her shoulders sinking, Ginny began to understand what an unbelievable fluke had occurred. Kirsten's past had come back at her with the force of a freight train, colliding head-on with the most poignant, irrelevant runaway train of fate.

"Does he know?"

She nodded. "But not until we knew Christo was missing. It just…it just happened that way." Ginny only knew about Christo's baby monitor and the sequence of events after that, none of the emotion, the tension, or of Kirsten's fears. "I couldn't tell him that first day, Ginny, and then things just happened so fast, or he was gone or we were interrupted or—"

"Oh, God," she said again, the lines in her sweet, round face deepening. "I'm sorry. The last thing you need now is me harping at you. How is he...what has he said?"

"Not much." Tears rushed into her eyes. "We have to find Christo first. That's the most important thing."

"Of course it is." Ginny swiped at tears of her own, carrying the weight of guilt that would never leave her. "Kirs, I'm so sorry—"

"Ginny, don't do that, please," Kirsten cried. "Please. No matter where we took Christo, they would have known. John Grenallo knew where Garrett had taken Christo right from the start."

"If anything happens to that child—" Ginny broke off.

Kirsten straightened. She had no such inability. She would tear out Grenallo's heart if she got the chance, but she had to believe it wouldn't go that far. She finished her tea, set the cup and saucer in the sink and stood looking out the kitchen window at the expanse of wilderness meadow and the surrounding forest. The quality of light struck her, the flatness of it. The sun must be directly overhead now, but the cloud cover blunted its rays.

Drawn by some instinct to examine the quality of light on the snow, she snatched up a coat of Ginny's from the pegs along the wall by the door, slipped into a pair of her friend's boots and let herself outside.

A few seconds later, Ginny followed, bundled to the hilt, but Kirsten's attention was riveted on the endless blanket of snow and she trudged beyond the area Sam had shoveled through drifts of snow for a better vantage point.

"Kirsten, wait. What are you doing?"

Shading her eyes against the flat glare of light, she stood a moment staring at the field of snow broken only by the tracks of a coyote. "Do you have a pair of sunglasses?"

"Goggles. Will that do?" Ginny tugged a pair out of her pocket with her mittened hand.

Kirsten took the orange-tinted goggles and slipped the elastic band over her head, fitting the mask to her face as she retraced her steps through the snowbank. Her breaths came out in small clouds, and it was mind-boggling how the altitude and snow slowed her pace.

"Kirsten...what is it?"

She studied the area leading away from the ground below Christo's bedroom window. "I don't know if it's my imagination or what, Ginny. Come here and see if you see this, too." She peeled off the goggles while her friend scrambled over the drifts. "Here. Put these on."

Ginny put on the goggles. "Okay. Now what?"

"Do you see depressions in the snow below Christo's room?"

"Some. Don't you think that's just the way the snow drifted?"

"Partly, but try letting your eyes follow the depressions leading away from the house. The light is so subtle now. I'm not sure you could see this at all in bright sunshine, but with the sun behind the clouds... Do you see what I mean?''

Shaking her head, Ginny removed the tinted goggles. ''I don't, but...are you thinking you could follow along, like a trail of bread crumbs or something?''

''I don't know.'' Kirsten shook her head thoughtfully. ''This light won't last. But if I could enhance the depressions with digital photos. Maybe.'' Tears rose up, foiling her resolve, exposing her house-of-cards emotions again. ''Am I crazy, Ginny? Deluding myself? Am I only imagining this could be useful?''

Ginny's eyes shone with sudden tears as well. ''If there's any chance at all, Kirsten, you should start right now. It's not like there are any more promising possibilities on the table. Come on. Get your camera. Get going.''

Kirsten swiped at her tears and hurried back into the house. Bypassing the dining room where Ann Calder sat with the men deep in strategizing, she went straight for her camera case atop the pile of luggage they'd left in the foyer.

''Kirsten?'' Picking up on her single-mindedness despite being involved in the discussion, Garrett got up from the kitchen table and followed her into the living room. ''What's going on?''

''The light outside.'' Kneeling on the carpeting, she pulled out her digital camera and reached deep inside for the special cartridge disks, hardly pausing to explain. ''I was just outside. It looks to me as if we may be able to follow the kidnapper's path through the snow.''

"Tell me how.'' He sank to his haunches beside her. An added urgency came into his voice. "Ten inches of snow have fallen since—''

"But there are depressions, Garrett, beneath the newer snow. I may be wrong. It may be some kind of optical illusion that I'm seeing, some anomaly of light, but if I can catch it on film—on the disk, actually, I might be able to use the computer to enhance the tracks.''

"You can do that?''

"I think so. But I have to get out there now.''

He reached for her, cupping her cheek in his hand, "You're brilliant, Kirsten.''

She swallowed hard. Brilliant was going to be a sad excuse if for all her cleverness, she couldn't track the kidnappers.

Chapter Thirteen

"We'll see."

She hurried back outside and took a couple dozen pictures on various trajectories outward from the house, taking her shots from different angles, from lying on the snow on her stomach to sitting, kneeling and standing, to catch different aspects of light. Inside again, not bothering to strip out of the layers of clothing she wore, she downloaded into the imaging software and went to work.

Garrett sat nearest her, but Sam and Ginny crowded around, along with Ross. Matt was long since gone, J.D. and Ann departing in a sheriff's vehicle only a few minutes before to start a house-to-house search for anyone who might have seen or have knowledge of a child missing and presumed kidnapped.

She first enlarged then digitally enhanced the photos, but it wasn't until she'd heightened the contrast of light to the maximum capabilities of the software that shadows faintly resembling the tracks of racket-shaped snowshoes appeared.

"Look! Look at this! Several inches below the

surface, the snow must have been heavier, its texture wet, almost dripping wet, then frozen. Is that right, Sam?''

''That's exactly what it was like,'' Sam exclaimed. ''The sheer weight of it dragged down the power and phone lines within the first four or five hours.''

But on the photo revealing the racket shape, it was impossible to discern tracks heading anywhere. Barely registering the discussion going on between Sam and Vorees behind her, Kirsten went from one to the next digital photo. As time had passed, the moisture content must have gone down significantly because atop the heavier pack the snow was much lighter and more powdery.

In the twenty-first shot, taken while lying on her belly in the snow, the single snowshoe shape extended into a line that went as far as the eye of the camera could see.

''Oh, my God, look! Look at this!''

''It looks like a trail to me, headed due north.''

''Garrett, this might really work! I've got to get back out there.''

''Okay, but slow down for one second. We've got to work this out. Sam, do you have a snowmobile J.D. and Kirsten could take to follow these tracks?''

''Yeah, but is it going to be possible to do what she's doing on the computer out in that cold with no electricity?''

''I can keep it inside my flannel shirt, keep it at body temp, anyway,'' J.D. offered.

''And I've got two spare batteries. Altogether enough maybe for four or five hours.'' She met Garrett's gaze again. "That's all the time we have anyway, isn't it?"

He nodded.

She looked to J.D. as well. "Do we have any better options?"

"Nothing as promising as this," he told her. "This gives us some direction. Anything else we do is going to be more haphazard."

"Let's do it, then," Garrett urged.

J.D. added layers of clothing from his flight bag while Sam, having only thrown on a coat, went out to the garage to fire up the snowmobile.

She studied the depth and direction of the tracks through the snow one more time to memorize what she could, then put the laptop into Suspend mode, closed it up and handed it to J.D. Ann laughed out loud at J.D.'s expression when Ginny produced Christo's miniature red corduroy backpack, adjusting its shoulder straps to fit over his head, fashioning an easy access pouch for the laptop.

But it escaped no one that the child's backpack straps lay within inches of the leather holster strap, or the juxtaposition of a machine pistol with Pooh embroidered on the corduroy.

Only Ann saw the glitter of tears in Kirsten's eyes. Huffing loudly, J.D. slid the computer into the backpack.

Ginny poured a thermos full of hot coffee and packed a plastic grocery bag full of homemade cinnamon rolls, then layered more clothes on Kirsten while J.D. chose the maps he wanted.

Within ten minutes the snowmobile was warmed

up and the two of them stood by ready to climb aboard.

Garrett took her aside. Snow crunched loudly under their feet. The sun peeked briefly out from the solidly overcast skies. He plucked off his glove and cupped her nape, emotion thickening his voice. "Bring back our son, Kirsten. Please. Bring him back."

THE GOING was more miserable than she could have imagined. With the temperature well below zero before the windchill, she grew numb inside of the first half mile—roughly the distance necessary to begin again. She had J.D. stop well short of the trees to reorient and took five photos on her belly, covering a hundred-and-eighty-degree arc.

He had the computer up again and ready for her download by the time she made it back through the snow.

By some intuitive dint of luck, the subtle indications of a path skirting the tree line showed up on the first photo. She went through the rest to make sure of the direction, and that there were not two sets of tracks splitting off, then worked quickly with the digital contrast.

"These are different." She pointed out a spot very near the trees where the depressions became significantly more narrow.

"The kidnapper must have changed over from snowshoes to skis here." J.D. oriented to his satellite photos, figuring the distance to be covered, talking aloud so Kirsten could follow the gist of his thinking about what had been in the kidnappers' minds. "The tracks head west-north-west here." He traced with his finger two destinations he thought likely, both over a ridge perhaps two miles away, noting on the map where the tracks would lead in each case. On the satellite photo, there wasn't much difference between the two, probably both the roofs of mountain cabins.

He lifted his binoculars, no larger than a deck of cards, to scan for any hint of a trail.

By the time they crested the ridge, Kirsten had spent a frustrating half hour trying to pick up on the trail that she could no longer make visible, and they were both too chilled to think clearly.

J.D. made the decision. They would circle wide and approach the cabin that was at least two miles beyond the other. "If Christo is in either one of those places, it's the one farther west."

He handed her the binoculars, and she saw why J.D. had made that seemingly arbitrary call. The closer of the two structures was covered with snow, no hint of melting on the roof, while on the farther cabin, the snow had melted around the chimney.

Four o'clock. Three hours left. By Kirsten's reckoning of the time they'd spent just getting to the ridge, it would take them another half hour to get to Christo, if he was there at all.

J.D. took another thirty seconds to call back and update Garrett, letting him know where they were and where they were headed.

Loehman still hadn't called to name the place and time for the handoff. Garrett was going slowly nuts, but her body numb with the subzero cold, Kirsten's heart began to race.

AT THIRTY-FIVE MINUTES after four, Garrett's cell phone rang. Guiliani, not Loehman, was on the other end of the call, his voice edgy. "Where are J.D. and Kirsten?"

Garrett leaned over the kitchen table to double-check himself though he knew to the degrees of longitude and latitude where J.D. had expected to be. He gave Matt the coordinates, then listened while he conferred with his CIA buddy.

Matt cleared his throat. "Did J.D. take a cell phone?"

"Yeah."

"Can you raise them?"

His chest tightened. "I don't know. Why?"

"You're not going to believe this, *paisan.*"

Impatient, his heart thudding, trying to keep cool, he snapped anyway. "Try me."

"I think I know where Christo is."

"Where?"

"A building on the north side of Jackson. It's closed up in the wintertime."

"How?" Garrett felt the plastic casing of his own cell phone giving way under his ferocious grip. He switched hands and forced himself to loosen up. "How do you know?"

"I don't know for sure, but the cell phone you gave the Wilders is there."

The cell on which Kirsten had tried for days to reach Christo. "You've got to be kidding me."

"Nope. I'm betting Christo stashed the thing in his duffel bag after the first time Kirsten called him. He probably messed with the buttons and turned off the ringer, or whoever's holding him would have found it and taken it away from him by now.''

"So, you've filtered out half a million other cells—"

"I can't take the credit, but yes."

"And you're saying Christo is trying to use it?"

"That's exactly what I'm saying. The signal's gone silent now, probably the battery's dead, but in the past six hours it's been pretty much a free-for-all for international long-distance calls lasting a couple of minutes each. My guess is they've left Christo alone in that building, he's found the cell again and he's been trying to call his mom ever since.''

Something fierce and tender, some emotion at once wildly grateful, proud and terrified gripped his throat at the thought of his own small son, alone, trying to reach Kirsten. Tears collected at the inner corners of his eyes and for a good long time he couldn't squeak out a word because he was hoping, too hard, that it was possible a four-year-old could do what Matt thought he was doing.

The alternative, of course, was that Loehman had crafted a nasty ambush.

"You there, Garrett?"

"Yeah." He let out his breath. "Even if I can't raise J.D., he should be calling in shortly. Tell your spook friend I owe him."

"Yeah, well, don't worry about it. Has Loehman called yet to tell you where to be when?"

Garrett swore. "No."

"Well, that's not a surprise, is it? You know he's not going to leave you time enough to vet the location."

"I know, but I don't have to like it." He was sorely tempted to go after Christo himself and deal with Loehman later. "How soon can you get to Christo's location?"

"It'll take a good hour."

"That's what I thought." He still needed the ex-spook's expertise in assessing photos downloaded from whatever satellite happened to be hanging in the night sky over Loehman's choice of a meeting place.

"Hang there another half hour," Garrett decided. "If our call doesn't come in by then, we'll have to forget it. Recovering Christo takes precedence. Get to him, check out that scene. Make sure we won't be taking Kirsten into an ambush. I don't know how soon she and J.D. will be able to get there, but assuming the rescue is a go—that Christo is even there, coordinate with J.D."

He rang off with Matt and punched in the number of the cell phone J.D. had taken. Vorees sat across the kitchen table from him, waiting to be filled in, his features harsh, forbidding as the granite Tetons.

Pushing redial every few seconds, Garrett knew the feeling well. It didn't help to be sitting here twiddling their thumbs waiting on Loehman's call. He filled in the few blanks Vorees had after hearing Garrett's side of the conversation.

Vorees cut loose with an angry, frustrated tirade.

"Take it easy, Ross," Ann urged him.

"You take it easy," he snapped. "Let me just say I would personally like to tear the son of a bitch limb from limb."

Ann ignored him. "Garrett, what would you think

if I went in for Christo? I'll get Ginny and Sam to take me…oh, except—'' she broke off, irritated at herself ''—that won't work because Matt has their vehicle and you'll need Ross's.''

Garrett nodded, chewing his lip. The highway patrol would come get her, but if Loehman's lackeys were watching their movements or Christo's location, a state vehicle could bollix the deal. He cursed under his breath. ''C'mon, Thorne, answer the damn phone.''

FROM HALF A MILE OUT, Kirsten's heart began to sink. From their vantage point above, approaching the mountain cabin with the snow melted around the chimney, she saw tire tracks departing the property. While that could mean anything, she worried that they were too late. Christo might have been there; he was probably gone now.

J.D. brought them as close as he dared risk the noise of the snowmobile engine, then helped her off the machine and down through the trees. He left her concealed behind a granite boulder thirty yards from the cabin, then moved, ran, half skidding the rest of the way to check it out first.

Her fears, however induced by the bitter numbing cold, proved dead on, once she was inside the cabin. There was no one in the house, only proof positive that Christo had been there. Off to the blind side of a naked mattress dragged in front of the fireplace in the great room lay the feather that belonged in Christo's medicine bag.

Panic knifed through her. If she'd had any energy left, it would have consumed her. As it was, she shot a dozen exposures of the place where Christo had been held hostage, then followed J.D. woodenly back outside where, in an outbuilding he broke into, he found a Jeep. He worked for ten minutes to hot-wire the thing before he gave up.

"I would really have liked it if just one damned thing could have gone right for us." He gave her a brief hug, ordered her to go back into the house where it was warmer and then took off up the mountain for the snowmobile.

She went inside and picked up the telephone to call Garrett but the line was dead. Ten minutes later, when J.D. skidded to a stop at the front door to pick her up, they learned the cell-phone battery was dead as well.

Swearing heartily under his breath, J.D. consulted his satellite map again and plotted a course to the western edge of town. He guided the snowmobile down the mountain road like a bat out of some frozen hell, swerving across the snow-plowed state highway to the first sign of life—a single-bay gas station. Naturally, the pay phone was out of order. Taking in J.D., the fresh-faced kid behind the counter offered up the station phone without a word and poured a couple of disposable cups of coffee.

J.D. punched in the numbers to Garrett's cell phone. He pulled Kirsten close enough and lowered his head so that she could hear as well.

Ann Calder answered. "J.D.?"

"Yeah."

"Where are you?"

"On the highway, a half a mile or so south of town."

"We've been trying to reach you for almost an hour. We know where they've taken Christo. We think he had the cell phone stashed in his duffel bag, that he's probably alone and trying to call Kirsten."

Her teeth gritted against crying out, Kirsten clapped a hand over her mouth as well, but the cry tore loose anyway.

"It's a town hall of some sort," Ann was saying, "usually closed up in winter. You're probably only ten minutes from it." Pulling herself together, Kirsten got out their maps to locate the building Ann described. "Matt is supposed to be there any second now," she went on, "vetting the place to make sure it's not some elaborate ambush."

"What about Garrett?" Kirsten asked. J.D. asked Ann.

"He left half an hour ago, right after the call came in." She described the meeting place Loehman had dictated. "It's a mountain lodge at the end of a private road off the county-maintained two-lane highway, roughly five miles up a canyon. Do you see it on the map? It's a T-junction, only one way to turn off."

Juggling her coffee, Kirsten spotted the road and pointed it out. J.D. answered. "Got it. What's the building opposite the turnoff?"

"A diner," Ann replied, "which is where Garrett and Vorees dropped me off about ten minutes ago. I've got company here."

Straining to hear along with J.D., Kirsten realized they'd dropped Ann there to watch who else came up that road, and that the "company" had to be her counterparts on Loehman's team. No one was going up that road.

"Was Loehman there already?"

"No. The road hasn't been plowed, and Vorees's are the only tire tracks. Matt's source says the place has to be empty, no signs of life or traffic in and out since before the blizzard. Since we know Loehman was still in Kalispell himself this morning—"

"He must be arriving in a chopper," J.D. guessed, and Ann confirmed that was their consensus. "Any idea," he asked, "when he plans to show up?"

"Garrett thought Loehman would let them cool their heels a while. An hour minimum, but God only knows. Hold on." Her line had clicked. "This may be Matt."

It was. He was on his way to the hall. J.D. peeled a couple of hundred-dollar bills out of a money clip, for which the station attendant was thrilled to hand over the keys to his pickup for a couple of hours.

From a rack filled with junk food, Kirsten grabbed a couple of packages of miniature chocolate donuts and boxed juice for Christo. Eight minutes later, at four forty-five, daylight all but gone, they pulled up alongside Matt, who sat in the Wilders' Toyota with the engine running less than a thousand feet from the hall, which itself sat up on a short road that was otherwise deserted.

Chilled to the bone despite the heater and coffee, her heart thudding, Kirsten rolled down the passenger window of the kid's restored 1965 Ford pickup as Matt rolled down his.

He gave her a thumbs-up. "It's all clear, Kirsten.

There's no one around. I don't know if Christo's in there, see, because the windows are heavily shaded, but we know it's warm inside and—'' he grinned ''—I just saw what looked like a flashlight beam making designs on the shades.''

Christo. Dear God, keep him safe.

Chapter Fourteen

Tears streamed down her cheeks.

J.D. downshifted and spun out over the icy road, skidding to a stop fifteen feet from the overlarge, double-wide door of the hall.

She bolted out her side and ran to the doors, calling for Christo, but there was no way she was getting in because the doors were padlocked. Beside her, J.D. unzipped his coat, jerked out his machine pistol and blasted the frozen lock to bits. Matt was there to shield her from flying metal, and to push open the door.

Both men edged inside, their weapons at arm's length and shoulder high, and plastered themselves against the wall to each side of the door.

Their precautions were unnecessary. Christo was completely alone, kneeling on a stage elevated no higher than one in a grade school, startled, frozen with fear and wild-eyed hope, the heavy flashlight waving wildly, catching her in its beam.

"Mommy?" His small, sweet voice trembled.

"Christo!" She flew across the dark vacant expanse and he crawled on all fours to the edge of the stage, dragging the flashlight with him till she met him there. Then he let it go and launched himself into her arms, his fierce expression filled with a four-year-old's rage at her for losing him, all mixed up with love and untellable relief.

When his dead weight grew too heavy, she sat his little bottom down on the stage. She couldn't get enough of touching him, of filling her gaze with nothing but her son, alive and healthy and true.

Garrett's son.

She swiped away her tears and steadied her lips against her fisted fingers. "Christo-man, did you think Mommy was never coming?"

"Those guys said you were coming," he offered, his wide eyes brimming with tears. His voice took on an altogether different texture, a little deeper, rounder. "To be honest—" his lips jutted in a heart-wrenching twist "—I didn't think you were *ever* coming."

Her emotions already strapped, already excessive and overblown, her heart began to pound. "What did you say, Christo?"

"I *said*—" he fumed at her, so in tune and uncertain of her reaction that his tears spilled out "—*to be honest,* I didn't think you were coming."

But Christo hadn't ever said "to be honest" in his short little life, or anything close to it. He'd picked it up from his captors. Sitting a few feet away on the stage, Matt had stiffened as well. She didn't even have to think when or where she'd heard it. Ross Vorees, when he ID'd the Identicomp photos of the Tacoma cops playing spooks across the street from her home.

She fought to keep control because Christo would go off the edge himself if she scared him even more now. She used his made-up Indian name to make her question seem playful. "Well, look, Crossing Bear, what color hair did the man have who brought you here?"

Christo brightened. "It was yellow, Mom. Just like Big Bird on'y more white, and real short."

Vorees. Ross Vorees. Her short, practical fingernails dug into her palms.

Blond, blue-eyed Ross Vorees was playing both ends against the middle in a bid for control of the TruthSayers.

In an instant she saw what terrible sense it all made, how Vorees had lobbied to come aboard Garrett's team, and suggested the kidnapping scenario. He was in a position to know where Christo was, and he exploited the knowledge when the moment was ripe to execute a real kidnapping.

Her throat clutched. She traded quick glances with Matt. It was obvious now that Vorees had offered up the names of the Tacoma cops staking out her house to make himself all the more credible, and he'd made sure Ann Calder was busy the night her snitch revealed Burton Rawlings's whereabouts at the bar.

Vorees stood sentinel that night, perfectly positioned to have shot Burton Rawlings through the window of the men's room, then "save" Kirsten's own life—though not until Burton made Kirsten aware of the existence of the tape backups.

Even in her emotion-riddled state, she saw clearly what Matt and J.D. knew as well. Ross Vorees couldn't lose. If he had his way, Loehman and Garrett would kill each other before the day was done, leaving Vorees in control of the TruthSayers. Garrett had gone to the meeting with Loehman. His only backup was Ross Vorees, the deadliest clandestine TruthSayer of them all.

She allowed herself one-half of a shaky, panicked breath, then looked straight into her child's eyes, seeing his father in Christo's features, and drew a long steadying breath. "Would it be okay with you, Christo, if I go find your daddy?"

His eyes flew wide. "Where is he?"

"Not very far from here, but you'll have to stay with one of our friends. This is Matt and J.D. Is that okay with you?"

Too excited to stand it, Christo jumped up and darted away, running full bore to the back of the stage where in his duffel was his medicine bag, and dragged it back. He dragged the medallion on its satin cord over his head and held out to her his daddy's lucky-charm medallion. "Take this, Mom," he ordered. "An' then come right back. *Right back.*"

Inside of thirty seconds, Matt and J.D. had rock-paper-scissored their way to the decision of which of them would take Christo back to Ginny and Sam's and stay with them, and which would go back with Kirsten for the snowmobile at the gas station, try to circumvent Loehman's security and get some semblance of real backup to Garrett.

Matt leaped up onto the stage, retrieved Christo's duffel and picked up his best friend's boy. "Come on, Christo. Let's me and you go baby-sit Wag while we wait for your dad."

KIRSTEN DROVE the pickup back to the gas station while J.D. studied the maps one more time, searching for a route through the frozen, snowy, moonlit night to the mountain lodge with only one way in and one way out.

By the time the attendant had helped her fill the snowmobile gas tanks, J.D. had his route and landmarks etched in his mind's eye.

J.D. wolfed down the last of Ginny's cinnamon rolls and they began. He guided the snowmobile back across the street, and once across, over a couple of miles of open terrain before taking the machine on a course to the rim of the canyon.

The engine seemed to Kirsten to roar rather than to drone, and she feared it could be heard coming for a hundred miles when by J.D.'s reckoning they were less than five miles from the lodge. Physically and emotionally depleted, she rested her forehead against J.D.'s back and let her mind go to a place where the roar was of silence, where she could feel the gratitude well up inside her for Christo's rescue, for his sturdy, steadfast resilience, and for his father, who might already have sacrificed his life to save the son kept secret from him so long.

She was in love with Garrett Weisz, and had been,

however mistaken she had been about his feelings for her, from the moment she laid eyes on him. And she understood now, at a level so deep that questions became meaningless, that when he told her she was mistaken if she believed it had been Margo he was making love to, he meant to say he'd been expressing a love only Kirsten deserved, that only she had evoked in him.

She'd been right about the most important thing. He was a man of honor; now she understood how honorable—beyond offering her a marriage for the benefit and convenience of their child, he held himself as accountable as he held her. He was right. Love wasn't going to be enough. He would be Christo's father no matter what, but they would have to find it in their hearts to forgive each other.

But now, descending from the crest of the canyon to the lodge, a hideously loud sound rent the air as a helicopter engine started up and the whine of its rotors began assaulting the air.

Unconcerned for their own noise now, J.D. sent the snowmobile hurtling closer and closer to the plume of smoke issuing from the chimney of the lodge, pale gray contrasting against the ink-black moonlit sky. Sooner than she expected, he braked powerfully and the machine stopped only a few feet short of the clearing, brightly lit by the chopper lights, thirty yards or so above and to the right of the front door.

More startling, Garrett walked out the front door, seemingly alone. Leaving the engine idling, J.D. hopped off, pulled his pistol and began skidding downhill, skirting into position to provide Garrett whatever cover he could.

She stripped off her mittens, pulled her digital camera up by its strap around her neck from deep inside her coat and went down on her belly, inching her way forward as Loehman and Vorees appeared.

The scene was eerily lit, her flashes would never be noticed. She began snapping photos as Garrett turned, spoke briefly to the two vigilantes, then turned his back and began to walk away alone in the direction of Vorees's vehicle.

A hideous premonition consumed her. The only reason Garrett would turn his back on Loehman was that he still trusted Vorees. Every instinct in her screamed she had to do something, had to stop this, had to scream at Garrett to get down before he took a bullet in the head and died without ever meeting his son. But even if he could hear her over the chopper engine, he would be dead before he could respond to her cries, and she knew J.D. was the only chance Garrett had.

Tears poured down her numb, frozen cheeks, but she did by rote the only thing she knew how to do. In freeze-frames through her camera lens she caught Vorees stepping back behind the man he would replace, raising his arm, pointing it not at Garrett's retreating form but at the back of Loehman's head. Before she could react or move her camera away or even cry out, Loehman dropped like a puppet cut from its strings.

A scream tore from her throat as she scrambled to her feet, but neither the shot nor her scream could be heard over the screaming pitch of the chopper engines.

She hurled herself down in J.D.'s path toward the clearing, screaming to Garrett as Vorees knelt, rolled Loehman's dead body over and exchanged weapons. Drawing a bead now on Garrett, he began to pull the trigger. Flying down into the chopper lights in the clearing, she screamed, then threw herself at Garrett, knocking him down in the split second before the bullet tore into the metal frame of the four-wheel drive at the level of Garrett's head.

Reacting with lightning speed, Garrett drew his own weapon, in the same motion rolling on top of her to shield her body from the gunfire. She craned her neck to see what was happening as Vorees went to one knee, braced and tried to get another shot off, but then shock crossed his features as not only Garrett's, but J.D.'s shots, ripped into his collarbone and chest in a tandem takedown. Fury and confusion crossed his cruelly handsome features in the surreal lights of the chopper on the vast white terrain as the impact of the bullets threw Vorees back without dropping him. He dropped his weapon, staggered to regain his balance, and then began to fall slowly, headfirst, facedown into snow.

The chopper pilot cut the engines and the lights, and the blades began to wind down to a slow, echoing *whap...whap...whap*. Garrett forced his forearms beneath Kirsten's shoulders and rolled over onto his back, taking her with him. His hands went to her frozen face, his fingers through her hair as he looked up into her face with only the light of the moon and stars.

"Kirsten—"

"Garrett…" Her tears, of adrenaline left over and starkest terror, changed to great spills of gratitude for his life, the life of her little boy's father, the man she had loved from afar for so long, miraculously spared.

Against all the odds. Against the maw of evil, the battle for the souls of men. The battle even his father, Kryztov, had scarcely survived.

For Christo, because of them, the world might yet be a safer, saner place.

"I love you." Her voice trembled, her throat ached with emotion too profound for such counterfeit things as words. His legs shifted around her, his body engulfed her and her heart swelled. "I have always loved you."

He lowered her face to his and nibbled away her frozen tears, his kisses more desperate than soft. The hard-core son of a freedom fighter was more tender than he had ever known himself to be.

GARRETT COMMANDEERED the chopper and its pilot to ferry the wounded and unconscious Vorees to the region's only hospital. J.D. and the pilot assisted the understaffed hospital emergency room in the transfer of their patient from the chopper to the operating room. Kirsten remained in the back of the chopper with Garrett and turned toward him on a bench seat behind the pilot's.

He took his arm from around her shoulders and

leaned back, resting his head, his hands on his thighs, his eyes focused away from her, neither close nor far away.

Steeped in emotions wholly unfamiliar to him, he felt himself raw and needy. "I'm glad Christo's all right."

She nodded. "Matt took him home to Ginny and Sam's." Her voice wavered. Garrett imagined more tears glittering in her eyes though he decided he daren't look.

"They didn't hurt him?" In his own voice he heard the shadow of threat, the echo of the man who had warned Kirsten McCourt not to mistake him for a soft touch. He hadn't reckoned with the sensation of finding himself so...exposed. It gave him a whole new appreciation for his own father.

"Christo was fine, Garrett," she reassured softly. "Miffed because it took me so long to come get him, but otherwise fine. He's the reason we knew you were in trouble."

He turned to her. "How?"

"He's at that age of parroting everything he hears—he's really got a great ear. He said something that made me think he had to have been around Ross Vorees. Christo confirmed it, really. He told me the man who'd brought him there had hair the color of Big Bird, only more white."

His heart swelled unmercifully, for his four-year-old son must be a chip off the old block when it came to innate detecting skills, but *he* didn't have a clue, any more than he'd had about a baby monitor. "What big bird?"

Laughter bubbled out of her; tears brightened her eyes. "You've got so much to learn, Weisz, that your head is going to hurt. You've never heard of *Sesame Street?*"

"Oh. *That* big bird."

"You faker."

"Yeah."

She took something from around her neck. "Christo wanted me to give you this." He held out his hand. His eyes fixed on the coin shape. Then, as he turned it over and over in the dim light, it dawned on him that this was the medallion of his own Gypsy great-great-grandmother, hanging from a bezel on a cord.

"Kirsten, does he know?" he asked, his voice low, urgent.

"What he knows, Garrett, is that when I come back, his daddy's coming, too."

Christo was going to love this. His daddy, coming to him in a helicopter.

WHEN THE CHOPPER set down in the front yard of the Wilder house, Christo flew out the door with Wag at his heels, and Matt in the wake of them both. He skidded to a stop and fell on his butt in the snow when in the harsh chopper lights he recognized Garrett for the man in the park.

His son's eyes grew wider and wider, his chin trembling fiercely. Garrett jumped down from the door of the chopper and scooped up his boy, who clung to his father's neck in a vise grip worthy of a professional wrestler.

Worthy of a boy, Kirsten thought, snapping photos of their reunion through her tears, who had believed his whole life that as soon as his superhero dad was done putting away the bad guys, he would come home.

Christo squirmed loose enough to turn to Kirsten. "Is he *really* my daddy?"

For one insanely long moment, with Ginny and Sam, Matt and J.D. and Ann Calder waiting for her answer, she looked into Garrett's eyes and then answered his son. "He is."

ON DECEMBER TWENTY-FIRST, Kirsten heard on a CNN news flash that Ross Vorees had been indicted in Wyoming for the murder of Chet Loehman. On the twenty-second, word came down that John Grenallo had been indicted on seventeen different counts mostly related to criminal conspiracy. On the twenty-third, Burton Rawlings died of the gunshot wound he had sustained.

On the twenty-fourth, Christmas Eve, she married Garrett Weisz in a small ceremony in her home on Queen Anne Hill. To be sure it was done right, Christo stood with the minister and watched them taking their vows to each other, and to him, pledging their love.

Garrett finally tore himself away from Christo's teepee on the stroke of Christmas Day. He went downstairs, then, and found his wife and thought how happy Christo's grandfather would have been, for he had survived Hungary in 1956, convinced that a man finally got what a man deserved.

It was a lucky man indeed who got both what his heart desired, and what he deserved. He stood at the bottom of the stairs, where there was mistletoe just pining to be invoked.

''Come here, Kirsten.''

Her eyes swam, her heart foundered. It was a lucky woman indeed, whose husband both honored and loved her for his own hero, who was the super-hero their son had always imagined, and the hero she had first met on a fateful night in the Mercury.

First Garrett, now J.D. and Matt!
Look for their stories in a new duet—

LOVERS UNDER COVER

by Carly Bishop
They're undercover cops hardened by their
jobs, but softened by the right women....
Available in

May 2000

NO BRIDE BUT HIS

June 2000

NO ONE BUT YOU

only from

HARLEQUIN®

I N T R I G U E®

If you enjoyed what you just read,
then we've got an offer you can't resist!

Take 2 bestselling love stories FREE!

Plus get a FREE surprise gift!

Get ready for heart-pounding romance and white-knuckle suspense!

HARLEQUIN®
I N T R I G U E®

raises the stakes in a new miniseries

THE McCORD FAMILY COUNTDOWN

The McCord family of Texas is in a desperate race against time!

With a killer on the loose and the clock ticking toward midnight, a daughter will indulge in her passion for her bodyguard; a son will come to terms with his past and help a woman with amnesia find hers; an outsider will do anything to save his unborn child and the woman he loves.

With time as the enemy, only love can save them!

#533 STOLEN MOMENTS
B.J. Daniels
October 1999

#537 MEMORIES AT MIDNIGHT
Joanna Wayne
November 1999

#541 EACH PRECIOUS HOUR
Gayle Wilson
December 1999

Available at your favorite retail outlet.

HARLEQUIN®
Makes any time special™

Visit us at www.romance.net

HICD

EXTRA! EXTRA!

The book all your favorite authors are raving about is finally here!

The 1999 Harlequin and Silhouette coupon book.

Each page is alive with savings that can't be beat!

Getting this incredible coupon book is as easy as 1, 2, 3.

1. During the months of November and December 1999 buy any 2 Harlequin or Silhouette books.

2. Send us your name, address and 2 proofs of purchase (cash receipt) to the address below.

3. Harlequin will send you a coupon book worth $10.00 off future purchases of Harlequin or Silhouette books in 2000.

Send us 3 cash register receipts as proofs of purchase and we will send you 2 coupon books worth a total saving of $20.00 (limit of 2 coupon books per customer).

Saving money has never been this easy.

Please allow 4-6 weeks for delivery. Offer expires December 31, 1999.

I accept your offer! Please send me (a) coupon booklet(s):

Name: _____

Address: _____ City: _____

State/Prov.: _____ Zip/Postal Code: _____

Send your name and address, along with your cash register receipts as proofs of purchase, to:

In the U.S.: Harlequin Books, P.O. Box 9057, Buffalo, N.Y. 14269
In Canada: Harlequin Books, P.O. Box 622, Fort Erie, Ontario L2A 5X3

Order your books and accept this coupon offer through our web site
http://www.romance.net
Valid in U.S. and Canada only.

PHQ4994R